Weekly Reader Children's Book Club presents

SWAMPFIRE

SWAMPFIRE

PATRICIA CECIL HASS

ILLUSTRATED BY CHARLES ROBINSON

DODD, MEAD & COMPANY, NEW YORK

TO MY MOTHER

SWAMPFIRE

1

SALLY WAS looking out of the train window, her face to the glass. Already the Virginia countryside was changing, from hilly land to long stretches of Tidewater pines, broken by clearings where the soil was sand. The train was chugging well away from Richmond, the big capital city, and heading east toward Smithfield, much nearer the flat coast.

As each mile went by, Sally felt herself leaving the tightness of winter homework and early bedtimes and rules, and coming closer to the open land that meant summer and being free. She pushed her light brown hair out of her eyes and peered into the trees, imagining Indians living there, left over from the Pamunkey tribe that was in Virginia long before nearby Jamestown was settled. They had known all about the land and the trees and the animals, and she had always wished that she could live that way herself. It would be much better than school.

But of course there weren't any Indians. Sally twisted around in her seat, turning blue-gray eyes on her brother, Andrew. He was two years younger, and he had the same light hair. But where she was small and slender, he was big and sturdy, and they did not really look alike at all. He was sitting behind her because he wanted a window seat too.

"You don't think Robin would forget about our camping, do you?" Sally said.

"Why would he?" Andrew said. "He was the one who thought of it. Besides, Cousin Anne must have told him we're coming. Say," Andrew pointed out of the window. *"Cyanocitta cristata."* He meant blue jay, but Andrew often used Latin words for birds. He was interested in science, particularly rock collecting and bird watching, and when he peered through his glasses and made an announcement people usually listened.

But Sally was still thinking of Robin. "He might have gone." She moved restlessly.

"Don't be dumb," Andrew said. "Cousin Anne would have written us. And where'd he want to go, away from the swamp?"

"I guess you're right," Sally said, and settled back on her seat.

No one in his right mind would ever leave a place

as exciting as the Great Dismal Swamp, she thought. Ever since they could remember, she and Andrew had been invited to spend their summers on Cousin Anne's huge peanut farm, and always, the swamp behind it had pulled them like a magnet. The farm's bottom pastures were separated from the first mild beginnings of the swamp only by a wandering stream, and each summer they had spent hours exploring there. Prickles always ran up and down their spines while they stood, big-eyed and silent, hoping to hear some distant twig snap and echo in the stillness. The past year or two they had grown bolder, crossing the stream and venturing a little into the swamp's wild passages. But they never went far. They knew enough to realize how easily they could get confused, how quickly they could be hopelessly lost.

Then, at the end of last summer, a lean and dark-haired boy had appeared one day while Sally and Andrew were at the barn helping the farm men milk. Come to borrow an ax, he had said. One of the men had given the boy the ax, and he had politely said "I thank you," and left as silently as he came. Sally and Andrew could tell from the boy's strange way of speaking, his dignity, and something solemn in his face that he was not one of the local farm boys.

They pressed the farm workman. "What's his name? Where does he live? Do you think he made those moccasins himself?"

This last question was Sally's. She had always wanted some real Indian moccasins like those the boy wore, not the kind she had, bought in a department store.

The workman had told them what he knew, which wasn't much. He thought the boy was from Tangier Island, where an isolated colony of English people had settled three hundred years ago on the other side of the swamp in the Chesapeake Bay. That would explain his strange way of pronouncing some words.

"I guess he lives in the swamp with his family," the farm man went on. "They're squatters, kinda, but they don't bother nobody, and your Cousin Anne, she let 'em stay. The father's got one arm that's useless, and the mother's all strange in her head. The boy's nigh on to supporting all three of them. I dunno about the moccasins, but people say lots of those Tangier Islanders got Indian blood."

Sally and Andrew waited eagerly for the boy to return the ax. He came back two days later. They had been lying against the milk house in the sun, eating figs, and they leaped up to smile at him. He walked over, gravely, and squatted down beside them, taking the figs they offered.

He told them his name was Robin, and they told him their names and asked him questions, shyly at first.

"Yes, my father came from Tangier," he said, his voice low and musical. "But now we live in the swamp. Have, ever since I can remember." He had made his moccasins himself, he told Sally, from deer hide.

"Did you kill the deer yourself?" she had asked, but he seemed not to hear, and stood up as if to go. But then, he had asked them if they would like to see a rabbit snare down by the stream, and they jumped up to follow him.

They talked that afternoon for a long time, dangling their feet in the water, and after that the friendship grew easily. They met often, Robin usually with something to show them—a figure he had whittled from a pine stick or a string of fresh-caught fish. Each time he told them some new thing about the swamp: where pokeberries grew, why crows had two calls, how to spot a fox's track . . . until all too soon it was time to leave the farm.

But on the day before they left, Robin made a suggestion.

"If you want to know the swamp," he had said, "next summer I could take you in a little way and we could make a camp."

This was a wonderful idea, and during the winter they had persuaded their parents that they were old enough to camp alone. After all, Sally would be twelve and Andrew ten, and Robin would be thirteen this summer. Cousin Anne, consulted by letter in the spring, had also agreed, with only a few reservations. The peanut crop was large this year, and she would have her hands full with that and the rest of the farm. "I know the boy, Robin—he did some work for me last fall, and again this spring," she wrote. "I've found him to be very responsible. As long as they promise to be very careful, it's probably a good idea—keep them occupied."

So it was all settled, and now it was June, and they were nearly at the farm. Andrew gestured out of the window with a sticky fist. "Look." The train tracks were curving eastward toward a long, dark line in the distance, black against the paler green of the farmland.

"Cypress trees!" Sally breathed, pressing her face against the window.

"It's the swamp," Andrew said.

They stared until the conductor appeared at the end of the car, calling "Smi-i-thfield STATION! Next stop!" Andrew got up to pull the luggage from the rack, his glasses slipping down on his nose. The last bag came down with a thump just as the little cross-roads station came into sight. They pressed their faces even closer to the glass, and before they knew it the train was creaking to a halt.

"There's Cousin Anne!" Sally said. The children rushed down the aisle and out of the train. They flung themselves at a stout, gray-haired woman accompanied by a huge Chesapeake retriever.

"Hello," Andrew shouted. "We're here!"

"And Delilah," Sally said, throwing her arms about the retriever, who wagged happily.

"It's wonderful to see you," Cousin Anne said. "Did you have a nice winter?"

"School," Andrew said.

"Chicken pox," Sally said.

Cousin Anne laughed and they all walked toward a battered-looking truck parked by the station house. The train gave a farewell toot and creaked away.

Cousin Anne opened the back of the pickup. "Put the bags in there, Andrew. My, you brought a lot!"

"It's mostly Andrew's bird and rock books," Sally said.

"And all your extra stuff," he retorted.

Cousin Anne laughed again. "Well, there's plenty of room for everything. I'll just run across to the feed store a minute, and then we'll be off."

Andrew picked up his field glasses, staring at some far-off birds. He couldn't tell what they were, and crawled into the back of the truck to get his bird book from his suitcase.

Sally stood still, staring around at the station yard. Bugs droned in the sun. A hound lay scratching his ear in the dust of the road that led to open fields. Sally felt the heat and thought how marvelous it was to be here. The station was a little distance from the edge of the swamp, but even so there was an elusive scent in the air, of cypress or juniper. It was a cool scent, of dark and mossy places.

". . . found it," Andrew said behind her. "They were cedar waxwings, *Bombycilla cedrorum*. Here comes Cousin Anne."

She was stopping to chat with two men crossing the station yard. Then she came to the truck and they got in. Delilah hopped in the back with the luggage.

"Now there's a lesson for you, children," Cousin Anne said, shifting gears with a lurch and bouncing out of the station yard. "Never believe everything you hear." She snorted. "Grown men, too. Still saying there's a ghost in the swamp. Never heard such nonsense."

They stared at her, feeling excitement explode through their veins.

"A ghost?" Andrew clutched his binoculars.

Sally leaned forward. This was better than any of the ideas she and Andrew had made up about the swamp all winter.

Cousin Anne shrugged. "Oh, people've been saying it for weeks now. Some great animal in the swamp, nobody knows what it is. Thundered out at Sam Bellows, walking on the swamp edge late at night, scared him half to death. He couldn't see what it was, but he said it was too big to be natural.

16

"Men went the next day, but bless your hearts, nobody found twig or sign. Of course no sign'd last very long in the swamp, when it's wet."

Delilah barked in the back of the truck, sounding happy. Now they had left the station and the crossroads behind, and the cool damp smell grew stronger.

"And then?" Sally prompted Cousin Anne.

"Then, a week after that, two men walked in about a half a mile"—Sally and Andrew knew that was about as far as most people went—"setting muskrat traps. Claim they heard a thrashing in the bushes fifty yards away, too loud for a deer. They didn't even try to stalk it, just left their traps and ran. Left four perfectly good traps too, so I hear."

"What do you think it was?" Andrew said.

"I wouldn't know, but ghosts are nonsense. Probably only some overgrown bear, or a big buck deer. Swamp fog'd make anything look like a ghost."

"Lucky ghost," Sally said, "living in the swamp."

"I don't call that luck," Cousin Anne said. "But I guess the place's got its spell. Swamp wild, we call it."

"It's awfully interesting scientifically," Andrew said.

"And beautiful," Sally said.

"I suppose, if you like land that wild," Cousin Anne said. "But all that thick mass of trees. Things in there nobody knows about, and never will. If you ask

17

me the place is a menace. I wish the government could clean it out, make it decent farmland. But they can't, it's too big. That swamp belongs to nature, probably always will." She smiled. "Anyway, you'll find out what it's like, with this camping you're planning. You *know* anything about camping?" She looked at them.

"Oh, yes," Sally said quickly. "Dad's taken us camping in the Blue Ridge Mountains. He showed us all about building fires and making beds out of branches and cooking."

"Well, you can't make beds out of branches in there," Cousin Anne said. "You'll have to sleep up off the ground. But I reckon that boy, Robin, knows what to do. Ought to, looks like he grows in the place."

Sally hesitated barely a second. "Robin's still around, isn't he?"

"Should be. I spoke to him about the camping trip when I got your parents' letter. He seemed pleased to know you were coming. At least, he smiled."

Andrew grinned at Sally in a superior way. "I'm always right," he said. "I knew he'd be." Sally was too relieved to be irritated at Andrew's tone.

"He's a good sort," Cousin Anne was saying. "Does everything I ask or better when he works for me. Never misses a day. I could trust him with any job, and find it well done. In fact, if I hadn't seen that side of him I wouldn't let you two go camping with him." She shifted gears again as she swung the pickup expertly around a pothole. "I could use him a lot more, but he says his folks need him. They practically live like Indians, I hear. It's a crying shame, too, if you ask my opinion."

"What is?" Sally said. She could imagine nothing better than living like Indians.

"Life Robin leads. Oh, I know he's looking after his parents, but they could go to a home. Mother not right in the head, lying in the hammock all day. Father hardly able to get about, with all that arthritis. And too proud to get outside help, like all those Tangiers. No, sir, that boy shouldn't be having to live in the swamp, all wild like. He'll go to seed. County authorities ought to help them find a decent home."

"He makes money, trapping," Andrew said hopefully from the window. They were nearly at the farm, running through fields of peanuts and then into a dark stand of pines. Suddenly Delilah bayed from the back of the truck, and everyone saw the flash of red, the fox sprinting across the road into the undergrowth.

Sally whooped, and Andrew banged on the truck door. Delilah's barking was frantic until Cousin Anne shouted at her, and even then the retriever continued to whine eagerly. The fox had excited everyone; seeing it, somehow, seemed to cut Sally's and Andrew's last ties with winter and school.

They kicked off their shoes as the truck turned into the stone gateway of Swamp Farm. The old brick house squatted under locust trees, its wide porch like a welcoming smile. Cousin Anne parked by a box-bush hedge and the children flung themselves out, all at once feeling so full of energy they ran down the lawn, the grass stiff and prickly on their bare feet.

Cousin Anne smiled. "When you've finished bouncing around, run on inside and change your clothes. We'll talk about your camping trip at supper, but you've got two hours before to find the boy and see what he's got in mind."

Sally and Andrew rushed upstairs to their little dormer rooms. The wide floorboards, the tiny windows fastened with wooden pegs, and old-fashioned washstands that held blue and white china bowls and pitchers were another world, a vacation world. Andrew tore open his suitcase and found his compass. He buckled it on his belt. Sally found her favorite pair of shorts, bought in a large Richmond department store instead of being woven by Indian hands, but they were nicely faded. She put them on and looked around.

"Have you got the signal mirror?"

"I've had it in my pocket all day," Andrew said.

Last year Robin had shown them how to make signals by flashing the sun with a mirror, and they had practiced during the winter. This would be the fastest way to let Robin know they were here.

Andrew found his pocket bird book, and they were ready. They ran down the back stairs. In Indian times it had been a secret passage leading to an underground hiding place. It was still dark and it still had a damp and spooky air.

When they stepped through the door at the bottom, onto the breeze porch at the back of the house, it was into a world so full of summer they could actually feel it. It came through their skin, a solid kind of heat that folded them into clover-soft air. It came through their noses: grass, honeysuckle, and the smell of swamp. It came through their ears: a great droning quiet, made more so by a distant hound's yelping, by a cow's moo somewhere behind the barn, and the nearby "hoo" of a mourning dove. Andrew pointed him out, flying off into the peanut fields that lay alongside the driveway. He looked into his book. "*Zenaidura carolinensis.*"

Far away over the swamp Sally saw another bird, sailing the air in ever-widening circles. "Look. A hawk," she said, feeling pleased. "Thank you, O Great Father. You have sent us an omen."

"Shut up," Andrew said. "It's just hunting for food." He hated it when Sally got silly; he always felt left out. "Come on," he said. "Let's climb the shed."

The highest spot on the Swamp Farm was a shed that housed the tractors. It perched on a knoll above the barn and it had been Sally and Andrew's favorite lookout for years. Andrew, who could run faster than Sally when he put his mind to it, got there first. He clambered up the swaying rail fence beside the shed, jumped, and caught the shingled roof. Sally pulled herself up behind him, kicking the air, and they went rapidly up the shingles on their stomachs, like crabs. At the ridge they sat down, spraddled on the peak.

"There it is," Sally breathed. Beyond the alders and the stream and the line of border pines at the foot of the sloping pastures, the trees of the swamp stretched east and south as far as the eye could see. So dark they seemed almost black; nothing marred their solid green wall. Heat rose in shimmers from hidden pools, and here and there vine-covered branches, taller than the rest, reached into the sky like clutching fingers. In the golden afternoon the swamp seemed to hum, pulling Sally and Andrew toward it.

Sally kicked the shingles, feeling shivery. "Do you think we'll see the ghost, when we're camping?"

"I'd like to know what it is," Andrew said. He pulled out the mirror and polished it against his sleeve.

"Maybe Robin will know," Sally said. Andrew turned the mirror toward the sun. Sally put her head down to see if he was aiming straight, and nodded.

The sunlight caught on the little surface, and Andrew held it there, sending light flashing toward the border pines. Three times he signalled, and then he stopped, and then three times again.

Sally saw the hawks, still circling above. Silently she asked the omen birds to make Robin see the signal, and come quickly. Andrew kept on flashing, three times and stop, three times and stop, but only a distant mockingbird answered his efforts. Sally's spirits were sinking. "Maybe he really has gone somewhere else," she said, easing her foot off a loose board.

Andrew didn't answer. He thought he had seen something. Yes, there it was again! A quick bright flash in the swamp, far beyond the border pines. "He's seen it!" Andrew said.

"There's another!" Sally had sat up. "It's nearer!"

Then they were slithering down the roof, dropping to the ground. They ran down the slope into the wide pastures, leaping cow paths and hummocks and panting through the grass. Finally they reached the shallow stream and splashed across.

Robin was leaning carelessly against a pine trunk on the other side, one foot against the tree. He smiled. "Hello," he said.

"Hi." Andrew grinned.

"Robin." Sally was unable now to believe they were really here, after the long, dark winter. She felt

23

shy. "I'm glad you came."

"I'm glad to see you too," he said.

"How did the signal look?" Andrew always wanted to improve his skill.

"Good. I saw it from far away," Robin said.

"We were wondering if you still wanted to take us camping," Sally said.

"Yes," Robin said. "I found a place."

Sally realized he had been waiting for them, after all. "Oh, that's marvelous," she said. "How soon can we go?"

"Tomorrow will be all right, if you can," Robin answered.

"Tell us what to bring," Andrew said, "We have knapsacks."

Robin looked vague, and Sally realized he probably never took anything with him—just lived off the land.

"We won't need anything," he said. "I have hammocks and fishing lines." He thought. "Maybe some extra matches, and—" he looked embarrassed— "do you have a flashlight? I have a lantern, but I ought to leave it behind for my father."

Sally realized he probably didn't have the money to buy a flashlight. "Dad told us to buy two at Shipton's store," she said. "And lots of batteries. We can get them in the morning." Robin nodded.

"Say," Andrew broke in, "do you know anything

about a ghost in the swamp?"

"So you have heard, already." Robin slid down to the pine needles, his back against the tree trunk. They crouched beside him. "Yes," he said, "I've heard people speak of a ghost."

"What is it?" Sally demanded. "Have you seen it?"

Robins' dark face broke into a smile. "You would never guess."

"What?"

"It's a horse," Robin said.

2

THEY STARED at him, not believing. A crow cawed, off in the swamp. It sounded wild and far away.

"A horse! But it couldn't be!" Sally found her voice. "How did he get there?"

"I don't know. But he's there," Robin said.

"But where? When did you see him?"

"A week ago. I was far up the stream." Robin pointed north. "I was in my canoe fishing, and I heard a noise. I looked up, and he was there." Robin rubbed his fingers along the pine bark, remembering that cool green day. He remembered the still water and the sudden "rat-tat-tat" of a woodpecker breaking the silence, and the way his flesh had crawled, when he knew suddenly that something was near him. Turning his head, he had seen a great shape, barely visible through a screen of branches. Then the branches had parted, and a horse had walked out onto the stream bank in full view. The boy had been too astonished to move, too amazed at the animal's force and beauty. For a moment they had been face to face, like two forest princes appraising each other.

"Go on," Andrew urged.

"He was very close. It was strange, but he didn't seem afraid. It was as though he came to see what I wanted. Then the canoe hit a snag and I had to look down. When I looked up again, he was gone."

"What did he look like?"

"Gold. Red-gold, the color of copper. He had a long mane, and his tail touched the ground. He looked . . ." Robin thought a moment. "He looked proud."

They were silent, thinking of a horse, a proud red-gold horse. The idea was so exciting it made Sally feel weak. "Of all the perfect things," she breathed.

"But what's he doing in the swamp?" Andrew said.

"He's hiding there, from a cruel owner," Sally said.

"You don't know he has a cruel owner," Andrew said. "He's probably run away."

"Maybe," Robin said, "but no one here's heard of a missing horse, or they wouldn't be talking about a ghost."

Sally shivered. "Isn't it dangerous for him? The swamp, I mean."

Robin smiled. "Spooks can float," he said. Then

he was serious. "I think he can take care of himself. He looks better than most horses."

"I'd give anything to see him," Sally said. Just then a bell boomed from the far-off house.

"That's supper. We've got to go." Andrew got up. "What time should we meet?"

"In the morning," Robin said. "I'll come to the house as soon after breakfast as I can."

Supper was enormous. They had ham and black-eyed peas with stewed tomatoes, and corn on the cob fresh out of the garden. Cousin Anne had fixed two platters of hot biscuits and there was strawberry jam, made that very day under glass, still warm from the sun. For dessert there was pecan pie and a huge bowl of whipped cream. Cousin Anne sat at the head of the table ladling out food and steadily refilling their milk glasses, and gave them what she called A Talk.

"You must remember that the Dismal Swamp is not a place to get careless in," she said. "I agreed to your camping on the edge because that won't be dangerous, and I know Robin won't do anything foolish. But—" and here she thumped the table with the edge of her hand— "I want you to promise me you'll use good common sense in there."

Andrew's lopsided talking-to-grown-people look came over his face. "You know we promise," he said, and Sally nodded.

"And be particularly careful of fire." Cousin Anne added.

"Fire? In the swamp?"

"Certainly," Cousin Anne said briskly. "The high ground in the swamp is full of peat—that's a kind of dry, flaky moss—and it burns very easily."

She got up from the table and they went out on the porch. She lit the mosquito candles and sat down in her big rocker. Delilah flopped by her side. The children climbed in a hammock. Beyond the locust trees, the night was black and hot and they could almost feel the swamp on the other side of the pastures, huge and alive.

"I remember a swamp fire when I was a child," Cousin Anne went on. "Lightning struck the peat. The peat grows deep in the ground and the fire gets down in it and burns for days and days. Then all of a sudden it bursts out, blazing, and the flames run wild." She rocked a while as though she were thinking. "The Indians didn't know about peat or understand how the ground could burn. They believed a swamp fire was a special kind of fire, and meant something special was going to happen."

The hammock creaked. Two pairs of eyes looked at her, in the flickering light.

"Mind you," Cousin Anne said, "I'm only telling you what the Indians thought. Don't go getting any silly ideas. Still, one thing's certain. A swamp fire's different from any other kind. Wilder, somehow. And if you ever saw one, you'd never forget it. Mercy!" she exclaimed. "Here I am rattling on, forgetting this is your first day in the country air. We'll pack you up right after breakfast, but now quick, along to bed with you!"

They went, not minding going to bed early; tomorrow would be here that much sooner. In their room they turned out the lights and lay in bed, listening to the country noises. Sally thought about the horse. She imagined him appearing from nowhere, on the stream bank, or running as though he were flying, free and wild, with his wavy mane streaming in the sun.

"Robin's the luckiest person in the world," she said.

"I don't know about that—" Andrew pulled up his sheet to keep off mosquitoes— "but he sure knows how to do a lot of things."

Sally was still daydreaming, and she was quiet for a while. Finally she said, "He'll teach us too. He said so." But Andrew didn't answer. He had fallen asleep.

The next morning the sun woke them, slanting red beams in their eyes. It was very early, only five-thirty, but Sally and Andrew were too excited to stay in bed, and they dressed and tiptoed down the stairs. Delilah rose from her rug to greet them, wagging her tail. They lifted the heavy bar from the double front doors.

"Um, good smells," Sally said, wrinkling her nose.

"Hmn," Andrew grunted. He was jumping around with Delilah. Sally knew it meant he agreed.

The grass and trees and sky were fresh green and blue, washed by the night. The sun was just touching the lawn, which was covered with white spider webs of dew. Sally and Andrew wandered across it, their footprints making dark trails in the silver green. They stepped into orange sun-paths, and followed one along the back of the house, where the old bricks smelled wet and cool. They went past the sheds and made their dewy trails beyond the barnyard, walking in waist-high weeds, soaking their shorts. Delilah bounded after a rabbit, lost it, and trotted back.

"Do you think we should take her camping?" Sally asked. "She might smell out the horse."

"Don't be so dumb. She's a retriever," Andrew said. "They just bring killed ducks out of the water. She wouldn't look for a horse."

Sally stuck out her foot but he dodged. "Well, it's true," he said. "Besides, she likes Cousin Anne. She wouldn't stay with us."

They came to the field fence; far off they saw the hawks again.

"I wonder if they're the same ones," Sally said.

"Probably," Andrew swung on the fence. "Hawks are jealous of their hunting territory."

Soon the birds drifted away, and Sally fingered a flower. "I love morning glories," she said, looking at them all along the fence, fragile and soon to die with the heat. "Such pretty colors."

"They're an interesting species of weed. *Ipomoea purpurea*," Andrew agreed. He rushed the fence, trying to jump it, and missed. He fell sprawling, and Sally leaned on the fence watching Delilah lick his face. She was thinking of the horse again, and somehow knew he could jump really well. She wondered what it would be like to be on his back, feeling the rushing wind, the rise to a timbered fence, the gathering power . . .

"Let's go and see the chickens," Andrew was saying. Sally followed him, and they looked for eggs, nervous of the angry clucking hens. One would not get off her nest at all and pecked at Andrew's hand, while Sally said "whoo." But it did no good and they left her, and in the end only found four eggs, large and brown.

"I hate to take them," Sally said, turning them over in her hand, feeling the still warm shells. "Think how the hens feel."

"They'll lay more," Andrew said. He found a basket on the shelf and put the eggs in it, to take to the house. "Let's watch the pigs."

It was feeding time and the farm men were calling, "Hargs, ha-r-r-gs!" Andrew tried it, too, but he couldn't get his shout loud enough. The men let them dump the feed buckets into the troughs, and they hung over the pigpen, watching.

"So fat," Sally said, "but they eat as though they're starved."

"Bacon," Andrew said unfeelingly, thinking of breakfast, "and ham, and pancakes with sausage."

"Sick." She threw a twig at him but her mouth watered all the same, and they went back to the house.

After breakfast Cousin Anne brought out powdered milk and cocoa and other packaged mixes.

"Robin said we didn't need anything," Sally said. "We're living off the land."

"That's right," Cousin Anne said, "you'll be mixing these with clean swamp spring water. But all campers have some supplies. Maybe Robin can't afford them."

They hadn't thought of that. "Well, not too many," Sally said. "We don't want to make him embarrassed."

"I'm taking peanut butter and cereal," Andrew said.

"And I suppose cream?" Sally felt like kicking him. Sometimes he seemed to be two people, one scientific and knowledgeable and the other an idiot who made her feel she couldn't rely on him.

"I've wrapped up corn bread and a chunk of ham and tomatoes too," Cousin Anne was saying, ignoring them. "Just in case you don't catch any food. Of

course you can always come home if you want anything."

"We won't want anything," Sally said. "We'll be
fine." But it seemed better to take the food than to
make Cousin Anne mad, and they added two little
containers of powdered orange drink and stuffed the
tomatoes in around the jar of peanut butter. On an
impulse Sally filled the last cracks of the knapsack
with two handfuls of sugar lumps, and Andrew
buckled it shut. They took the second knapsack and
sat on the floor with their things around them, putting them in and taking them out because nothing fit.
Sally said she felt like Francis Marion.

"Who's he?" Andrew said.

"He was some man in the Revolution, who was
always having to choose what to take with him. He
rescued people away from the English by hiding in a
swamp. It was in South Carolina, I think." Sally's
history was a little vague, but she had always liked the
story of Francis Marion because his nickname was
"The Swamp Fox."

Finally they put in extra socks and thin rubber
boots, the kind that went over their shoes, their tooth-
brushes, the bird book, and matches. They added
three tin plates and spoons, forks and knives, and
three tin cups. They put in some soap for washing
their clothes when it was sunny, and a collapsible
pail. At the last minute they borrowed a small pair of

Cousin Anne's clippers, for vines, and a can of bug spray. Andrew's binoculars and compass went on his belt, and Sally put the signal mirror in her pocket. They were ready just as Robin came around the house, a neatly wrapped bundle of hammocks and rope slung over his shoulder. He had a small ax at his belt.

"We've done everything except get the flashlights." Andrew ran down the steps to greet him. "We can do that on the way."

They loaded each other up and said good-by to Cousin Anne. "Be back here the day after tomorrow to check in," she said. "I'll want to hear from you every other day so I'll know you're still alive."

"Of course we'll be alive," Andrew said. "These knapsacks are so full, all we could die of is broken backs."

"And remember that an ounce of prevention is worth a pound of cure." She got in the last word.

"What does that mean?" Andrew said as they walked down the driveway.

"It means if you see a queer looking sandy place you should walk around it instead of going through and ending up stuck in some quicksand," Sally said.

Robin laughed. "She's right."

At the gates they turned right on a dirt road that ran through the farm's fields until it came to a store, a mile away. Originally the store had been a boat landing on the swamp canal at the end of the farm property. Later it had added gasoline pumps and general supplies, and a post office window for the farms in the surrounding country. This morning its yard looked deserted except for two chickens pecking at the dusty ground. But Robin stopped suddenly, pointing at two empty cars, parked beside the frame building.

"What's the matter?" Sally said.

"One of those cars belongs to the game warden. I don't want to go in."

"I'll go, then," Andrew said matter-of-factly. "I'll get some popsicles, too."

"Good idea," Sally said. "Get nut crunch, if he's got it."

Robin took Andrew's pack and pushed into some prickly bushes at the side of the road. Sally followed him, and they settled down to wait. It was very quiet. The birds had stilled and the cottontails had found shade in the gullies, for the sun was dropping heat over the land like a blanket. Robin crouched on his heels, thoughtfully chewing a leaf and watching the white sand road.

Sally scratched her elbow and found a ladybug, and flicked it away. She watched it land on a twig over her head and crawl along, and wondered how it would feel to be that little, and have all the fields to crawl and fly in.

She realized Robin was looking at her. She smiled, but he was solemn. "I hope you don't mind waiting here," he said, "but I can't see the game warden because I hunt and fish in the swamp for my family, and I don't have any money to buy the license. He came to my house one day when I wasn't there, and looked everywhere for signs of game. He'd really like to ask me questions."

Sally nodded.

"It's the warden's job to know who goes in and out of the swamp," Robin said, "and what they do there. He can read the swamp signs, and once I was careless."

Sally looked at Robin with new admiration. "How far have you been into the swamp?"

"Farther than most people," he answered.

They heard a car door slam, from the direction of the store. "Do you think the warden's being in the store had anything to do with you?" Sally asked.

Robin shrugged. "He might be posting a notice, or checking who's rented boats for the swamp lately. Who knows?" He shrugged again. "Andrew will tell us."

But Andrew was taking a long time. Perspiration trickled down Sally's back and made her itch all over. She shifted a branch away from her ribs and thought about the popsicles, and her mouth watered. If he takes much longer they'll melt, she thought, and then

37

she jumped. The undergrowth was rattling, a little distance away toward the store.

"That's only Andrew," Robin said. "He thinks Indians walk in the brush instead of the road."

Sally giggled. Andrew had a lot to learn in silent woodcraft. But when he burst into view they stopped laughing. His face was red, his glasses awry.

"They're going to chase the ghost!" he gasped out. "They've heard about it, and the warden's in there hiring an extra boat from Mr. Shipton to go after it, and find out what it really is!"

Robin jumped up, not even seeing the popsicles Andrew thrust out. "You didn't say anything?"

"Of course not. I just bought the flashlights and listened. I waited until they left so I could hear everything. They're starting this afternoon."

3

"Do you think they'll find him?" Sally looked at Robin.

"I don't know." Robin sounded worried. "They could."

"But they'll be in boats," Andrew said. "And a horse can run anywhere he wants to."

"That's right," Sally said, hating to admit it. "And he's awfully smart."

"The warden's smart too," Robin said, handing Andrew his pack. "They may not stay in the boats."

Andrew struggled into it. "Well, let's go, anyway," he said. "If we get into the swamp to our camp maybe we can see something."

"Which way did the warden go?" Robin asked.

"That way," Andrew waved his arm back toward town.

Robin swung across the road, Sally and Andrew close beside him. They went into the cornfield on the other side, kicking up dust as they walked through the tall rows.

"Where does that canal go?" Andrew asked.

"Off to the east," Robin said. "I haven't been on it much."

Andrew reached in his pocket as he walked. "Maybe it's on this map."

"Where did you get that?" Sally said.

"At the house," Andrew answered, handing the map to Robin. "It's pretty old, but I thought it might be useful."

Robin looked at it. "Might be, but I'd a lot rather trust my own head than any map," he said.

They crossed the cornfield and entered a strip of pine woods. Robin turned, going through the trees at an angle. The pines grew close together and the branches were low and thick, but Robin seemed to slip through them as though he were oiled. Once he got out of sight ahead, but they caught up, and found him waiting at the edge of a wide stretch of marsh grass. It was shoulder high, brushing their arms and legs. Little frogs hopped aside at their every step, bugs flew zinging off the tops of the grass, and Sally thought nervously of snakes. But at that moment Robin whispered, "Look!"

They peered around him and saw a huge black

and white bird standing ten feet ahead on a flat mud bank. It saw them at the same time and launched itself with great flapping wings, sailing away down the marsh like a dignified kite, its long feet dangling. They watched until it flew out of sight around some trees.

"He's always in this place," Robin said. "We surprised him."

Sally took a deep breath and looked around, her fear of snakes melting away. We're here, she thought. We're here. The sun felt hot on their heads and the ground was warm and black under their shoes. "Yippee!" Andrew said suddenly, pulling some grass and letting go. It swung back, quivering.

Robin looked startled. "You'll scare every animal away," he said, but then he smiled, and they knew he felt the same way.

They slogged through the grass until they came to a big thicket. Honeysuckle vines grew all over it, filling the air with sweet scent. If Robin had not been leading, pushing aside the vines for another opening, twisting his way through the tree trunks to find tiny little paths, Sally and Andrew would have been hopelessly lost. But they followed close behind him, watching his every step, and ten minutes later he brought them out at a stream.

"It's the same one that goes along below the farm pastures," he said. "We're just farther along it."

The stream had made a horseshoe bend and in the curve, almost like an island, was a little clearing. Sally and Andrew looked around with delight. The ground was mossy, and to one side there was even a bubbling spring.

"It's good water," Robin said. "I drink here a lot, and animals use it too."

He showed them tracks in the black mud beside the spring. They were tiny, like the tracks of little hands. "A raccoon," Robin said. "He was here last night." He pointed to a stone by the spring, smeared with mud and leaves, where the tracks were jumbled. "That's his washboard. Coons wash their food before they eat it, the way people do."

Sally and Andrew peered into the elderberry bushes beyond the bank, hoping to see a dark creature stealing along. But the coon was well hidden, sleeping away the day, and they gave up and followed Robin to the center of the clearing. They put down their things.

"It's a perfect camping place," Sally smiled at Robin. "No wonder you thought of it."

"What should we do first?" Andrew said.

Robin unbuckled his ax. "We need wood," he said. "I'll chop some."

"What do you want us to do?" Sally said.

"It's all right. I'm used to doing the work myself," Robin said.

"But think how much faster it'll be if we all help," Andrew said, peering seriously through his glasses.

Robin looked pleased. "I guess you're right," he said. "You could make the fireplace, and get kindling."

Sally and Andrew set to work, clearing a sandy spot for the fire. Robin said the best kind of fireplace was a shallow pit, so they dug one out, about six inches deep, with their hands. They found some flat stones and set them around the pit in a circle. They collected all the loose sticks and branches they could find, and stacked them in a pile near the fireplace. When they had finished, Sally brought over the knapsacks and Andrew went and watched Robin, who had chipped a ring on a big dead tree, which was still standing up at the edge of the clearing. Robin's swing was steady and accurate, and the groove in the tree was getting deeper and wider with surprising speed. Finally Andrew couldn't stand it. "Can I try?"

Robin stopped. He was dripping sweat. "Sure. But be careful." He showed Andrew how to grip the handle and stood with him until Andrew got the feel of his stroke. "Don't swing too hard or too far," Robin said. "That's when you miss and hit your leg." He explained how to strike the blade at an angle, so it wouldn't glance off the wood, and how to chop around only one side until the tree was ready to split. Andrew tried, and after a few uncertain strokes he

43

began to get the hang of it. He took turns with Robin, chopping until the tree was bouncing back and forth in the ground. Then Robin gave a mighty whack, and the trunk splintered in two.

"Here's our table," Robin said, pointing to the big stump end. "We can chop fire logs from the rest of it whenever we need them." He smiled at Andrew. "You're getting good."

It took all three of them to wrestle the big chunk out of its place and roll it over to the fireplace. Robin planed off its top side with the ax, and Sally began putting some of their things on its flat surface.

"Do you suppose the Indians made their camps like this?" she said.

Robin shrugged. He wiped off the ax blade and put it away. "Making camp, you look for water and grass and open space. It's the same for everybody, Indians or us, unless you're hiding. Then you camp in thickets and don't make fires."

"Is anybody else hungry besides me?" Andrew asked.

"We brought some food with us." Sally looked at Robin. "I hope it's okay. Cousin Anne made us."

"That's fine." Robin didn't seem insulted at all. "We can eat it now."

"It won't be any good tomorrow, anyway," Andrew said. "Food decomposes."

"You always say that so you can eat more," Sally

said. She got out the tomatoes and corn bread and the hard salty ham. They took it all over to the stream to cool themselves off, and ended up sitting with their feet in the water. Sally looked at the green wilderness around them.

"Was the place you saw the horse anywhere near here?" she said.

"Not far." Robin got up and pulled back some drooping bushes. "I was in this."

A canoe lay half out of the water, blending so perfectly with its surroundings that at first it was hard to see.

"Cool," Andrew said.

Their eyes picked out its outlines, and they could tell it was made of some kind of hide, tightly stretched over a wood frame that had been bent and curved to a graceful shape. Sally thought it looked like a delicate toy, except that it was bigger.

"Did you make it yourself?" Andrew asked. Robin nodded.

"How did you learn?" Andrew leaned forward and ran his fingers over the smooth wood frame.

"I made two bad ones first," Robin said. "Finally I got this one right. I always keep it here." He let the branches drop back, and slid it into the water. "Get in. I'll show you where I saw him."

They stepped over the sides, settling carefully on the bottom, and Robin pushed off into the stream. It

46

was clear and brown and full of sandbars, and Sally said, "We could go all over the swamp like this."

Robin grinned. "We could, but we're not. Your Cousin'd have a fit."

"She wouldn't mind. A horse is a bigger thing than being mad."

"Well, we don't have to go very far. That's the place. Over there." He pointed beyond a sandbank, and drifted up to it. Andrew was in the bow and he jumped out on the sand and looked into the bushes. But there was not a sign of a horse. There was nothing in sight except trees and water.

"Well, I guess we knew he wouldn't be," Andrew said, getting back in.

"He could always come back," Sally said.

"Maybe," Robin said. "But I don't know if he's around here any more. I'd have seen him." He began backpaddling. "We better get back now. We've still got the hammocks to hang."

They drifted back through the dappled shade, and landed and hid the canoe. Robin picked out a large pine tree at the edge of the clearing, and he and Andrew shinnied up the thick trunk, the hammocks wrapped around their waists. Farther up there were sturdy branches jutting out like the spokes of a wheel, and they could climb like monkeys, high in the air. They tied the hammocks in a close circle, while Sally stood under the tree and watched. "That one's not straight, the far end's sagging," she called. They waved, and changed it. Coming down they dropped from branch to branch until the lowest one. From there they leaped, and landed with two thuds.

"Camp's done," Robin said, looking around the clearing. "And sun's dropping. It's time to fish."

They hunted for bait, little white bugs that lived under leaves or rotted logs. When they had a dozen or so, Robin baited the hooks and they crawled out on a white cedar that lay in the stream. "Don't talk," Robin whispered. "Just drop in your lines and jiggle them every now and then."

It was very still. The air and the water and the sky seemed all in one. But suddenly Andrew's line jumped, shattering the placid surface, and he leaped up.

"Stop jerking!" Robin hissed. "Sit down and pull!"

But he was too late. The line was limp.

"Darn," Andrew said. Sally thought he was going to hit the water.

"Try again," Robin said. "He may come back."

Andrew sat down without a word. He baited his hook and dropped his line in again. This time he was like a statue, and minutes later the fish hit again. Andrew lifted a flapping, silvery creature out of the water.

"It's a speckled trout," Robin whispered. "Hold a few minutes now. We don't want to scare away the rest."

After a little while the fish began to bite again. Eventually they caught seven more, all speckled trout. Robin cleaned them, and Andrew watched. He liked to dissect things and see their bone structure, but Sally felt sick at the sight. She went and dangled her feet in the water, watching the daylight fade. A mockingbird sang on the other side of the stream and a fish jumped nearby, making a splash. If only they knew where the horse was, she thought, and what he was doing. He was probably coming silently out into a stream like this to drink, his red-gold coat standing out against the green, and he was . . .

"Hey, we're ready to cook," Andrew called. Sally jumped up and ran over to the fire.

Robin put water in the pan for lack of oil, and laid in the fish. Sally put corn bread and plums on the tin plates, and in no time at all the fish were done, brown and crisp on the outside, and flaky and white on the inside.

They ate until they were stuffed, and finished off with powdered milk. Then everyone lay back on the moss, groaning, until Andrew slapped a large mosquito on his arm, and another on his leg. "It's my freckles," he said. "I think they attract mosquitoes."

"Get the bug spray," Sally said.

"We'd better get in the hammocks," Robin said. "In a few minutes they'll be out in swarms."

They rinsed the plates in the stream, slapping wildly at the ever-increasing stings. Hastily Robin led the way up the pine tree, and with relief they found the mosquitoes did not follow. It was hard getting into the hammocks, which seemed to give way alarmingly at the touch. But eventually everyone was settled, hanging in a close circle, high in the air.

"I love it here," Sally said, wriggling around.

"Like cocoons," Andrew grinned, pulling his hammock around him until only his face showed. "I'd never have thought of it."

"You never should sleep on the ground in the swamp," Robin said. "If you don't have a hammock, you should pudge out a hollow log with a stick and sleep there."

"I like hammocks better," Sally said, thinking of snakes. "Oh, look at the moon."

It was rising above the tops of the pines, enormous and white. It was so big it seemed almost alive, throbbing with some mysterious force that made them want to reach out and touch it. Imperceptibly it moved upward while they watched, icing the land with silver, lighting the clearing like day.

"Now we may see something," Robin said. "Keep as still as you can."

Sally and Andrew hunched into comfortable positions and settled down to wait. The silence was so heavy you could almost hear it, as though the swamp were holding its breath. An owl called across the stream, and mists began to rise.

50

Suddenly Robin nudged them. "Look over there," he whispered.

A deer stood in the clearing. It had appeared from nowhere, a statue silvered by the moon. It turned its head and then a tiny fawn cantered out of the trees, followed by another. The fawns ran in circles on the grass, playing, so delicate they seemed unreal.

The three in the tree watched spellbound while the doe lowered her head to nibble at tender shoots. The two fawns imitated her, but quickly grew tired of that and began to play again. Then a stick cracked beyond the stream, and suddenly the deer were gone.

"Oh-h-h," Sally let out her breath in a long sigh. "How lovely."

"What do you think could have scared them?" Andrew whispered.

"It could have been anything," Robin whispered back. "Deer are very flighty."

They settled back again. The mists were rising higher and Sally watched them. Idly she thought they looked like streamers of smoke under the moon. It's a good thing it isn't smoke, she thought. That would mean the swamp was on fire. The idea made her shiver, in spite of the heat. A fire, blazing and burning, no way to stop it. Red and gold, the color of— she sat up suddenly, and a bird flew out of the tree, startled. What a perfect name for the horse! Swamp Fire! Blazing and burning, a fiery steed . . . "Listen!" She told the others.

"I like it," Andrew said. "It's a good name."

But at that moment Robin hissed.

"Shh! I hear something!"

They froze.

"Don't you hear it?" he whispered.

"No, what?" Andrew said.

The silence was suffocating. They could hear nothing, except a rising chorus of frogs and crickets, and the blood pounding in their ears. And then, far off, distant and haunting, they heard a high yapping.

"That's funny," Robin said softly. "It's a hound."

"Sounds like it's in the swamp," Andrew said. "I thought that was against the law."

"It is," Robin answered, "except the warden uses hounds sometimes, finding game that's old or sick."

"Then what do you think . . ." Andrew began, and stopped. For suddenly he knew. They all knew, and were struck with horror. The warden was in the swamp already, and he was hunting the horse with hounds!

"Oh no!" Sally moaned. "What can we possibly do?"

4

Several miles away, deep in the swamp near a large natural meadow, the warden was also listening to his hound. He was standing in a stream, his flashlight making an eerie arc under the black trees.

"That dog's picked up something unusual, all right," he said. "He wouldn't bell like that on deer."

"Might be a bear," said the man who was with him.

"Might be," the warden said. "But then again, he just might be onto something we don't know about." The warden reslung his rifle, which had been knocked askew by some low-hanging branches. "I'd like to kick myself for letting him slip his leash like that. Not a chance of catching up with him now."

"Best we get to open ground and hope he runs the critter, whatever it is, in a circle," the other man said. "Good moon up, plenty of light to shoot by."

"Right."

They started along the stream, the water slopping against their hip boots. In fifteen minutes they were at the edge of the open meadow. It looked empty and smooth under the bright moonlight.

"Now I don't hear the dog," the other man said.

"Mmm," the warden frowned. "You better go back to camp and get the others, and bring the rest of the dogs, too."

"Okay," the man said. "We'll be quick."

He departed in the direction of their camp. The warden unslung his rifle and moved into cover. He crouched on his heels and settled down to wait.

The hound was a quarter mile away. He was winded already, for he was running fast, nose down on a fresh trail. When the hound had gotten a fresh puff of it on a breeze, he had slipped his leash and shot off in a wild chase.

His quarry, a bobcat, was going fast, zigzagging through a reedy, vine-matted morass and jumping the choked slit of a stream. The hound stopped baying, saving his breath. He worked his way through a cane brake and came out on the other side. Ahead lay the meadow again, and he quickened his pace. He began to give tongue again, high wild yips.

Ahead, under the black trees at the meadow's edge, Swampfire was standing motionless. A few minutes before he had doubled back on his trail, just in time

54

to see the bobcat flit past like a gray ghost, routed from his night's hunting by the dog's pursuit. Almost as soon as the cat had gone, the hound burst into view, baying frantically. Swampfire, nostrils wide and trembling lightly, held perfectly still. He watched while the dog came on, a dark loping shape in the moonlight, and ran by. Then Swampfire moved out into the open.

The warden saw him, over a quarter mile away. For one breathtaking instant the horse stood there, a huge chestnut creature with a flowing mane and tail. His chiselled head with its keen sculptured lines was high on his powerful neck. The great sweep of back and shoulder and the deep girth between his forelegs spoke of speed and power and heart. The warden's eyes narrowed, and he shifted his gun. "What in the world . . . ?" he said. "A horse!"

Then the hound gave tongue again, turning on his circle, and Swampfire, uneasy, began to run. He was coming toward the hidden warden. His muscles rippled in the moonlight like molten gold, his fine long legs seemed to float over the high grass. He plunged across a tiny pool, breaking the phosphorus water into a thousand flashing fires. He splashed out again, easily gathering speed. Now he was running as though he were flying, sweeping down the meadow like a rushing wind.

The warden ran out, trying to block Swampfire's

path. The moon went behind a cloud, and in the half light it was hard to see. By now the horse was nearly on top of him, looming huge in the dimness. The warden raised his arms. He lunged for Swampfire's forelock but he missed, and a second later the horse was gone.

Sally and Andrew and Robin stayed awake long after the hound's baying had died to nothing in the distance, huddled in their hammocks, their voices low. "At least the hound didn't catch anything," Robin said. "I could tell by the way he sounded."

"I hate just sitting here, not knowing what's happening." Sally grabbed her knees and rocked back and forth.

"Well, we shouldn't just sit here," Andrew said. "We've got to do something."

In the moonlight Robin hunched up in his hammock. "Maybe I could get us over there," he said. "I think I know where they are, now. Just about where the baying was coming from is a big wild meadow. It's all dry ground with lots of grass. I should have thought of it before, but it's been a long time since I've been there."

"Lots of grass!" Sally said. "The kind Swampfire would eat?"

Robin nodded.

"He *could* be there, then!" Sally said. "And that

Robin nodded again. "That's what I think, too."

"Of course, we don't know—" Andrew looked thoughtful—"what the hound was chasing."

"No, but suppose it was Swampfire," Sally said. "Or he's there, anyway."

"The warden will find him," Robin said.

Sally moved sharply, and her hammock jiggled. "We can't take a chance like that," she said. "We've got to go and at least look for him, now that we know a place to try."

"Right," Andrew said. "And if he's there we've got to find him before the warden does." He turned to Robin. "How do we get to the meadow?"

Robin explained that farther down, the stream joined an abandoned canal that had once been used for logging. If the canal wasn't too overgrown by now, they could get to the meadow in the canoe.

"When should we start?" Sally said.

"As soon as it gets light," Robin answered. "Right now we should go to sleep."

He curled down in the hammock without another word and closed his eyes, and soon Sally and Andrew could hear his regular breathing. Sally wondered how he could possibly drop off to sleep like that when she and Andrew were still so wide awake, but she decided to try, and she lay down too.

But in a few minutes she sat up again. It was impossible even to feel sleepy.

"Andrew?" she whispered.

"What?"

"Let's look at the map."

He fumbled in his pocket until he found it, and they held it between them and studied it by the flashlight. They saw the canal Robin was talking about, and some others with funny names: Jericho and Portsmouth to the north, Five Mile and Feeder to the east. Some of the canals led to a huge lake called Lake Drummond, that seemed to be right in the middle of the swamp. There were places marked "bog" or "wild orchids," and another part said "Gum Section . . . Copperheads." Much of the map was blank, and these spaces were marked "unexplored."

"There's no meadow on here," Sally said.

"This map's so old it wouldn't show," Andrew whispered. "Look, it's dated 1910. A meadow'd be grown up in trees by now, or underwater."

"That means those canals are old," Sally said. "Who do you suppose built them?"

"I don't know," Andrew said. "Those guys in the old days who did things. They were always building canals to get places."

They put the map away and watched the moon sail slowly across the sky. Finally they began to doze, first in fitful spells, and then at last they fell into a deep sleep. Hours later the moon sank in the west, but the swamp stayed dark until a sudden breeze swept across the stream, bringing the pungent scent of dawn.

Robin sat up, and shook himself. He wiggled Andrew's hammock to wake him. "The crickets have stopped," he said. "We can start."

"What time is it?" Sally felt as though she'd hardly closed her eyes.

Andrew held his watch under the flashlight's beam. "Quarter to five."

Andrew and Sally climbed carefully down behind Robin, seeing nothing except the moving flashlight, feeling pine needles brushing their faces, then slippery smooth under their feet. Under the trees the clearing was like a cave. The pines enclosed the air in a heavy, black stillness, where nothing seemed to be moving except themselves. They heard occasional sounds: the far-off "plop" of something falling into water, the distant whistle of a bird, a cracking branch.

Sally held the flashlight while Robin and Andrew packed one knapsack with matches and fish hooks, peanut butter and packages of Instant Breakfast mix. On top went the collapsible pail, and at the last minute Sally remembered the sugar lumps and put them in her shorts pocket.

They ate quickly, bread and pieces of ham washed down with powdered orange juice, and just as they finished, the darkness started lightening into pale gray. Robin eased the canoe from its hiding place, floating it forward like a silent leaf on the dark water. He put Andrew in front with the ax and a coil of rope, Sally in the middle with the knapsack, and then he pushed off and hopped in the stern. He picked up his paddle and began to stroke, evenly and steadily. It was quiet around them while the world slowly turned into day, and they saw a land so green and alive that it seemed to be pushing each leaf and blade visibly toward the sky.

"Oh-h-h," Sally said. "Look at those sky colors."

"I'd feel a lot better if we could hear the dogs again," Andrew said. "At least we'd know what they were up to."

"You're sure they didn't catch him?" Sally turned around to Robin.

"I'm sure. Hounds make a terrible racket if they catch something. More snarly-like." He was concentrating. "The canal should be just along here." He saw a place where there was a dent in the bushes and headed for it. They pushed into a small passage that looked as though no one had been through it in years.

"Duck down," Robin said, and Sally and Andrew put their hands over their heads against the stinging branches, while Robin half pushed and half poled the canoe. The bushes whacked against their backs and then they came out into the canal, and everyone breathed again. At least in this part, the canal was navigable.

"I knew it," Sally said. "It was seeing the hawks."

"What hawks?" Robin asked.

She told him about the good omen, and he smiled. He seemed more carefree today, and Sally guessed it was because they were heading into the swamp. Or maybe, she thought, it was because they were getting more used to each other.

The canal seemed deeper than the stream had been, and Robin handed his extra paddle to Andrew. Instantly they picked up speed, slicing rapidly through the still water. The sun was peeping up now, sending deep gold rays through the trees, lighting the surface of the water. The water was an unusual shade of dark brown, and Sally couldn't resist dipping in her fingers, watching it foam softly under her hand. She thought it looked like cola, pouring into a glass.

"It's a funny color," she said.

Robin pointed at tall juniper trees along the banks. "That's from those trees. Their roots grow in the water and they make it brown. It's good for drinking, though."

"The people at Jamestown learned about juniper water from the Indians." Andrew sounded like he was giving a speech. "They put it in their ship barrels because it keeps pure a long time."

"You always say things like that," Sally said. "You don't know they're true."

"Want to bet?" Andrew turned around and the canoe dipped.

"No, but I'd like to see the book you read it in."

"Okay, if you want to go back to school right now and get it," he said scornfully. He knew he was right because since Jamestown was near the Dismal Swamp, he had liked that part of the history book and he had remembered it.

"Well, I don't," Sally said. "But I'll look it up next fall." She didn't want to think about fall and school so she dropped the argument, staring instead at the canal banks.

They were constantly changing, now high and covered with gall bushes or bristly with pokeberries, now lower, screened by lacy willows. They seemed like dikes, holding back a sea of green. Andrew saw a hermit thrush, which he said was a very shy kind of bird that people almost never saw. But this one, tan and white speckled and sitting right out in plain sight on a branch above the canal, never even stopped his lovely song when the canoe passed under him.

"He doesn't act a bit shy," Sally said.

"Maybe he doesn't know we're people," Andrew said. "I'm getting excited," he added, and they knew what he meant. It was marvelous to see a bird that might never have seen any people before.

Soon the thrush's song was muffled by the greenery, and suddenly a violent rustling, quite close by, made them all jump.

"I think it's mostly reeds and water in there," Robin

said. "Too wet for the horse. Probably a deer."

"Whatever it is, we surprised him," Sally gloated, feeling woodsmanlike.

"Not enough to see him," Robin grinned, teasing her.

After a little way the canal began to twist and turn. Branches and vines dropped low overhead, making it a green tunnel. Here and there a water lily floated peacefully in the cool gloom, white against the amber water. Robin warned them to watch for snakes on the trees and told Sally to stop trailing her fingers over the side.

"They could be in the water too," he said, and she snatched out her hand.

They rounded a bend and Andrew, leaning out, reported from the bow that the going was getting worse. The lilies were much thicker, and Robin was forced to go slowly, trying to pick open lanes. The trees were tightly laced overhead, and the air felt oppressive. Paddling grew more difficult, and drops of perspiration began to show on Robin's face. He leaned over the side and splashed his face and neck with water.

"Want to trade places?" Andrew offered.

"No," Robin said. "But take the ax and cut a path in front. Sally can use the knife."

They made more progress this way but even so it was slow work. They chopped doggedly, hanging out of the canoe, edging forward. Sally thought of the lily pads in the fish pond of their garden in Richmond, used by six gentle goldfish for an umbrella. She wondered how she could ever have thought they were so lovely and harmless.

"Hey, there's a big wall up ahead," Andrew said. He stood up gingerly, to see better. "Try going left. Maybe we can get around it."

Robin turned the canoe, but as they drew closer they saw that a solid mass of old logs and brush stretched a foot above the surface all the way across the canal.

"It's a beaver dam," Robin said. "An old one. Otherwise they'd have eaten all the lily pads."

They came nearer and Robin pointed out another mound of sticks at the edge of the stream. It had been the beavers' house, called a lodge, but it was empty now. They struggled through a last stretch of lilies that was like white and green matting on top of the water, and reached the dam. It was solid underneath, but sticks and branches poked up from its surface like spikes. Robin brought the canoe carefully alongside and they got out, looking for places to stand on the crunchy top. When they found footholds, they picked up the canoe and carried it, staggering, across to the other side.

"Whew!" Andrew was dripping wet. "One rip and we'd have had it!"

Robin looked a little bit worried. "The meadow shouldn't be far," he said, "but I hope it doesn't get any worse."

They got back in. The water looked stagnant. Reeds grew out of it, and green scum seemed glued along the edges. The canal was much shallower, and in places they had to use their paddles for poles.

"What we need is an airboat, like they have in the Everglades," Sally said. She had seen one on a television program and she had wanted to ride in one ever since.

"I saw a swamp buggy once," Robin said. "But I didn't like it. It was too loud."

Just then, the canoe lodged in some reeds and wouldn't come loose. They poled hard, rocking it back and forth.

"Hey, is that noise the hounds?" Andrew said.

They held still. Sally brushed her hair out of her eyes. "Yes," she said. "It is."

"Wait." Robin was studying the sound. The dogs were yapping in fits and starts, far off to the right of the canal. "They're all in one place," he said. "That means they're still in camp. We're ahead of them."

He slipped overboard and stood in the water, tugging gently until he freed the canoe. He felt under the bottom to make sure the hide wasn't damaged, and walked a little way in front. The canoe rode higher without his weight and he stayed in, pulling the bow. The water was up to his knees and a murky dark brown, and suddenly he jumped back in the canoe.

"Water moccasin," he said. "See him?"

They caught a quick glimpse of what looked like a piece of thick black wire whipping along the surface. "Wow!" Andrew said.

"Keep poling," Robin said. "He's gone."

They went another fifty yards and then the canal deepened. The boys began to paddle again and they swung easily around a big floating log. They were all concentrating on the water, and no one noticed that the trees were opening up on the left until Andrew looked up. "Hey!" he said.

"It's the meadow," Robin said. Then he added, "Shhh." He stopped the canoe and cocked his head, and they were quiet while he listened and looked. It was almost as if he were smelling the breeze. But there was no sign of danger; this part of the swamp seemed deserted. The dogs' barking had died away, and except for the constant calling of the birds, nothing broke the silence of the golden, sunshiny morning. They crept forward again, hugging the bank, gliding silently over the water.

"Over there," Robin whispered, motioning at a sand spit that jutted from the bottom of the bank. He put the bow right onto it, and Andrew jumped out, pulling hard.

Robin scrambled up the bank first. He motioned them up, and they lay on the top beside him and peered over. An empty expanse of tall grass bordered by trees stretched out of sight. Already they could see it was beginning to show little heat waves, shimmering upward in the sun. "What a marvelous place to ride," Sally said, wondering what it would be like to gallop down it, feeling Swampfire's shoulders moving under her, huge and strong beneath her legs.

"Where do we start?" Andrew said.

"Not in the meadow," Robin said. "It's too open. We'll have to split up, one on either side. And one of us should stay at this end, to watch the canal."

"Okay," Sally said. "Whoever finds something can signal with the mirrors."

"No, they're too visible," Robin said.

"Why not bird calls?" Andrew suggested. "Bob white. There're not too many in the swamp, but it's the only one Sally can do."

She hit his arm. "Shut up."

"Do it," Robin said.

She spit out the leaf she was chewing and tried. It was quavering but clear and Robin answered her, such a perfect whistle that Andrew's jaw dropped.

"Boy, how'd you learn to do that?" he said.

"I don't know—just hearing them, I guess," Robin answered.

They started back to the canoe for their things. At

67

the canal Robin dipped for water, but he made a face and spit it out. "It's still stagnant," he said. "I saw a spring back in the meadow. We better fill our canteen there."

"I'll do it," Sally said. "You and Andrew can bring the stuff." She got the canteen and disappeared over the bank. Andrew and Robin pulled the canoe out of sight under a thick clump of woodbine and followed her up the bank with the pack and the ax and a coil of rope. They heard Sally struggling through the high grass and suddenly, her urgent whistle. Robin leaped into the meadow and Andrew came running behind. He saw Sally standing by the spring, staring at the ground. The water was bubbling in the black mud at her feet, and beside it lay the perfect, rounded hoofprint of a horse.

5

"IT'S FRESH," Robin said. "You can tell by the water in it. Still oozing. And there're more." He pointed.

"He's here!" Sally said. "Come on, hurry!"

She darted off, following the other tracks.

"Sally, will you stop it?" Andrew said. "You always do that. We can't just rush up on him. We've got to plan."

She turned around, feeling silly.

"He's right," Robin said. "We've got a good chance now. Swampfire must be really near, and the hounds are way off yonder."

He looked carefully at the tracks, trying to find a straight trail. They showed plainly in the mud around the spring. But each time he found one trail and followed it, it led into the meadow and disappeared in the dry grass.

He came to a halt. "This won't work. We'll have to split up, the way I said before. Andrew, you go back and wait at the canal. Swampfire's not in the meadow or we'd see him, so Sally and I'll each take one side, and try to pick up his tracks under the trees."

Andrew nodded. He left them, heading for the bank, and Robin cut the rope in two halves with the ax and coiled one for Sally. Then he helped her line up the compass. "You can't get lost if you don't go too far into the trees. Keep the meadow in sight."

Sally was chewing her hair, barely able to hold still from excitement. "Okay," she said.

She left almost before he finished talking, and Robin was alone in the hot sun. He began to walk across the meadow, listening to the silence. His eyes roved the grass and the trees in front of him, looking for a telltale flicker of chestnut, a flash of movement, anything to give a clue as to the horse's whereabouts.

He saw two deer ahead under the branches, browsing peacefully on twigs, flicking their tails. When he came closer the deer stood looking at him, absolutely fearless.

He knew a spotted fawn would be somewhere nearby, melted into a thicket. The thought pleased Robin and he smiled. The sun was high, the sky was blue, the black earth was springy under his moccasins. He could think of nothing better to be doing than this, looking for the horse . . . Swampfire. Sally had drew always seemed to think of good things. He liked the way they talked, arguing and stopping and making friends again, like puffs of clouds that blew across the summer sky. Sometimes he thought they were going to hit each other, but a minute later they were laughing again. He wished he could be like that.

He heard a whistle, thin and squeaky. Sally. He peered across the meadow and could see her waving under the trees. He ducked low and scooted across, almost hidden by the tops of the grass. Sally was pointing at a line of tracks in the soft ground beside a gooseberry bush.

He bent over to examine them, then quickly straightened up again. "Deer tracks. And old." He looked at her. "But that was pretty good, noticing them."

"Have you seen anything?" She covered her pleasure, feeling swollen inside with the praise.

"Not yet. But we will. I know he's here." He left her to go back to his side of the meadow, and she started on.

Andrew was having a marvelous time at the canal. He could keep watch and also collect rocks at the same time, and in only a few minutes he had seen seven different kinds of birds. He liked being on his own. It gave him time to think. He already had had some new ideas for next year's biology class. He stooped to examine a rock more closely, thinking it might be coal. It wasn't, and he tossed it away. Three redwing blackbirds flew up under his nose and he watched them go off across the meadow, and then he saw a weasel on the canal bank, the first one he had ever seen. He used his binoculars, getting a good look before it slipped away. It was getting hotter as the sun climbed higher, and he had to wipe his glasses frequently. He saw the hawks, high in the sky, floating on their lazy circles.

"Sally's omens," he said to himself, wondering if they really brought good luck. Suddenly he stopped in his tracks. On the other side of the canal he heard the hounds baying again. This time it was close by. His heart started to pound as the baying came and went, muffled in the undergrowth and trees. While he was trying to tell which way it was moving the sound stopped, abruptly. Andrew turned around to look down the meadow through his binoculars, but there was no sign of Robin and Sally. He wasn't certain what to do. Should he try to find Robin? Or signal? He didn't want to bring them back here if the hounds were coming. He waited another two minutes, but still there was only silence. Andrew eased along the canal bank to the trees at the meadow's edge. There was always the chance that if the hounds were coming this way, they might be driving Swampfire in front of them. He had better move out, but still be close enough to see.

Sally had not heard the hounds, and neither had Robin. They were much farther away than Andrew realized, pushing aside bushes, creeping around tree trunks, looking everywhere for a flash of red gold in the green. All Sally had seen since the deer tracks were three rabbits, and no other animals seemed to be moving at all. Even the birds had stopped their endless chirping and calling, lulled by the midday heat. Perspiration ran down Sally's back, making her shorts slide around her waist as she walked. The bushes felt dry against her hot skin and her feet were burning in her shoes. Her legs were itching. She stopped and wiped her face on her sleeve, watching a squirrel who was chattering at her from the top of a bush, almost as though he wanted to talk.

"Why don't you tell me where Swampfire is?" she said. Her voice frightened him, and with a flick of his bushy tail, he ran up a tree trunk and disappeared. Sally giggled. "You're on the warden's side," she said.

She stooped down to dislodge a pebble that had somehow gotten inside her moccasin. She couldn't reach it and sat on a log to pull off her shoe. Before she started on, something made her look sideways into the gum trees, and she felt suddenly cold all over.

She was looking straight into the face of a wildcat. He was as big as Delilah, except that he was silver and gray, with little black spots all over him, like a huge pet tabby cat. He was standing with one paw on a dead rabbit, and suddenly he hissed, a loud spitting sound. Sally grabbed her moccasin and slid backwards. She scrambled to her feet and ran, not daring to look behind. When nothing landed on her shoulders she ran faster, darting through thickets and tangles, looking for anything that might hide her from those snarling teeth. Her heart was pounding so hard that it was several minutes before she realized the wildcat wasn't following her. She stopped, and leaned against a tree, almost hugging it for support until she got her wind back, and the thumps inside her died away.

"Um-m-mph," she let out her breath in a whistling sigh. She waited a little while longer to make sure the wildcat really wasn't coming, and then she put her moccasin on. She straightened up and looked around, wondering what to do next. The ground here was damp and sandy between patches of water. Sally looked down, planning which way to walk back, and she couldn't believe what she saw. In the sand beside her left foot were four hoofprints.

She had almost been standing on them. They were exactly like the ones back at the spring in the meadow, but these weren't jumbled up. Sally walked carefully ahead until she found more, and followed the trail across more sand until it entered the gum trees again.

The trees in front of her were growing in a large grove with open aisles between. It was hard to see in the dimness, but when her eyes focused, she gasped. Fifteen yards in front of her, stepping into a shaft of golden sunlight that pierced the gloom, was the most beautiful horse that Sally had ever seen. Tall, powerful, his silvery mane and tail thick against his bronzed reddish coat, he seemed almost to glow against the dark trees.

"Golly," Sally breathed, not daring to move. Thoughts tumbled through her. Can he see me . . . will he run . . . can I catch him . . . should I signal Robin? No, she thought. A whistle, even her best one, might not fool the horse.

Slowly she edged herself to one side. She flattened down on the ground and wormed to the shelter of an elderberry bush. She could no longer see Swampfire, which meant he couldn't see her either. Sally bit her lip, her mind racing.

Surprise was her only hope. He had moved away from her into what appeared to be an open glade. Somehow she had to get close enough to get her rope on him before he knew she was there. The ground between them looked terrifyingly unsafe. It was swampy, with little humps of grass between dark pools of water. It might be possible to hop from one to another, like stepping-stones, but the thought made Sally shudder.

She crept off to one side, keeping behind bushes until she was safely across a tiny bog. But at the next one her foot slipped and she nearly fell into horrible, sucking mud. She grabbed a branch and hauled herself forward. Instantly she stopped, terrified that Swampfire might have heard her.

But he hadn't, and she started forward again. A cluster of trees lay ahead, and Sally had to squeeze past their trunks. She passed a screen of holly, wincing as their sharp leaves pricked her arms and legs. She crept forward until only a thick clump of bushes was between her and the horse. She undid the coil of rope from her belt and stayed still, listening. Beyond the bushes nothing stirred, and only the far-off song of a thrush broke the silence. Cautiously Sally edged her way through the bushes. She peeped through an opening in the branches, her heart thumping.

He was only ten feet away. Framed in the circular green opening, she saw his head and shoulders, the chiselled nostrils flaring, the dark eyes, the tumbled, silvery forelock. He sensed something, she could tell. He turned slowly, testing the silence and the air. Suddenly he whickered, and Sally's heart gave a thud. He knew she was there.

He took a step toward her, and Sally ached to reach out her hand, to touch his silken neck. Hardly realizing what she was doing, she came out of the bushes. They stood looking at each other for one

- 77

long instant, and then the moment broke. The horse was snorting, backing away. Sally began to edge sideways, her hand holding out the sugar, the other clutching the rope. If she could just get a little closer . . .

But Swampfire wheeled. His powerful hindquarters bunched, his long forelegs pawed the air. In a few great strides he reached the edge of the glade and trotted into the trees.

Sally ran after him. "At least he's not running," she thought. Across the glade she found his tracks in the soft earth. She followed, stumbling over logs and through thickets, safe as long as she stayed exactly in his hoofprints, but getting steadily more out of breath. She couldn't keep this up much longer. She circled a pool that he had jumped, and edged around a fallen tree.

To her astonishment Swampfire was standing a little way beyond, looking back as though he were waiting for her. Sally stopped, and backed up. His dark eyes were watching her. Suddenly, he turned around to face her, and whickered again.

"You want the sugar!" Sally said. She held it out in her hand. "You did see it! You weren't going to leave this, were you? Oh, you're beautiful." She began to back up, talking softly.

He watched her. He kept whickering, one hoof digging the ground. Then he took a step forward, and another. He began to move faster, muscles sliding under the golden coat. She slowed down, and he kept coming. She stopped, and he walked on, until he had come all the way up to her and lowered his head to her hand.

He snuffed her palm, and picked up the sugar with his velvet lips. He crunched it, and she could tell he liked it. Carefully Sally slid her rope under his neck, then up over his mane. He jerked back, quivering. "Whoa-oa-a, whoa-oa-oa," she said.

But he was bunching his hindquarters, ears back, and she stopped. She gave him more sugar, and slowly, slowly, she tried again, and this time eased the rope around his neck. Her heart in her mouth, she tugged. He didn't move. Then she realized she was so nervous, she had hardly pulled at all. She tugged harder, and he took a step forward. The rope around his neck was not a very good way to control him. She wished she had a halter.

Sally looked around desperately, wondering where Robin was. She had gotten a good distance away from the meadow while she was running after Swampfire, and now she couldn't see it at all. Panic froze her for a minute, but then she remembered the compass; she got it out and steadied it. Robin had said the meadow was south. Yes, there, the needle was holding steady on N, and she gave a strong pull on Swampfire's rope and set out in the opposite direction, toward S. Swampfire walked so quickly she was almost running, patting him and talking to him. Then she saw the meadow through the trees—it hadn't been far at all.

"We're going to surprise Robin," she said to Swampfire. "He's not going to believe it!" She wanted to jump on the horse's back and feel him rush across the meadow like a flying bird, but instead she whistled softly, her throat feeling dry.

On the other side of the meadow Robin stopped short. He heard Sally's whistle, and he answered. Then he saw her. She was coming toward him with Swampfire beside her, a rope resting lightly around the horse's powerful neck. The horse was even more beautiful than Robin remembered, and he ran forward. "How did you do it?" he asked.

"It wasn't so hard," Sally said. "He's not wild. I mean, he's not tame either, but he knows about people, and sugar."

Robin walked around him, admiring the arched neck, the depth through his chest, the flat slim legs. "He's fine," he said. "He's not a horse from a farm."

"He's beautiful," Sally said. Her heart was still thumping from excitement. They had found him. They had found the horse. This beautiful, golden creature, standing huge and alert beside them, was theirs. Nothing, Sally thought, would ever be the same again.

"He hears something," Robin said.

Swampfire had thrown up his head and was looking down the meadow, toward the canal.

"What?" Sally said.

Then they saw it too, a moving figure, with a pack on his back. Andrew. He saw them and waved. "I heard the hounds near the canal," he panted when he reached them. "You found him! My gosh! What happened?"

Sally told him, still so excited she could hardly talk.

"That was really good, thinking to bring sugar," Andrew said. "We might never have caught him without it."

There was a burst of baying near the place where they had left the canoe. "They're coming," Robin said.

"They'll see him," Sally said.

"My gosh," Andrew said. "What'll we do now?"

6

"GET HIM in the trees," Robin said. "Quick. Out of sight."

They led Swampfire under the maples just as the warden came into sight down the meadow, tall and wearing a khaki uniform. Two men were with him and three hounds were in front of him, running around in circles and making little yips. Two of the dogs were brown and one was black and white spotted.

Robin peered through the branches. "It doesn't look like they know we're here," he said. "Did they see you?" He looked at Andrew.

Andrew shook his head. He felt proud of the way he had crawled over the bank, then slid down and crouched, running that way until he was too far away to be seen. "I don't think I left any footprints,

"Good," Robin said. "Then we've got a chance."

He pushed farther into the trees, and Sally and Andrew coaxed Swampfire after him. At first the horse swung wide on the rope, uneasy, but Andrew edged to his other side and he swung back. Finally he moved along with them, still skittish but willing to follow.

"I think he's been lonely," Sally said.

"He won't be any more, now we've found him," Andrew said.

"Neither will we," she said.

Robin went back to the edge and watched the men, eyes narrow against the glare. "They're making circles," he said. The dogs were following hand signals, swinging on wide arcs in front of the men, into the trees and out again. They were spread out, and sniffing everywhere.

"We've got to get in the water, and cover our tracks," Robin said. He led them all the way through the grove until the ground sloped down and grew soft. Ahead lay flat black water, standing between the trees.

"In there," Robin pointed. "It's not deep."

He splashed in, going up to his knees. At the edge Swampfire half reared, but Sally and Andrew held on to the rope and urged him down with little tugs. The bottom was firm, covered with a layer of matted leaves and old twigs. It looked as though nothing had disturbed it for a hundred years. Except snakes, Sally thought. Could there be alligators? No, they only lived in Florida. The dogs sounded nearer and she forgot her fear. Everybody ran, pulling Swampfire into a trot, their feet sending showers of crystal water into the sunlight, soaking their clothes and the horse's belly.

Once Andrew risked a glance backward, and saw nothing but trees. Robin was leading them straight into the swamp on a zigzag course, circling wide around every shallow place that might show their tracks. But still the dogs kept baying, louder now. It sounded right behind.

Sally was almost out of breath. She tried not to slow down. She felt she would rather have a heart attack than stop, and wondered briefly what it would feel like to have one. She would fall to the ground, gasping. . . . She was looking at her feet and she ran right into Robin, who had halted to listen.

He was panting too. "I *wish* they'd stop running around." He sounded mad. "They're too close. They might find us by accident."

He found an almost impassable thicket and forced a path inside, and Sally and Andrew followed him with Swampfire. In the middle they were completely hidden.

"Keep Swampfire here," Robin told Sally. "Don't let him move. That'll keep his scent from carrying."

She wondered if she could do it, but she nodded, and Robin beckoned to Andrew. They ran back the way they had come, one hundred, two hundred yards. Then Robin stopped, well out in the open.

"We'll wait here," he said. "Just stand still."

Seconds later the dogs bounded into view. They were apart, running around sniffing, but when they saw the boys, they instantly bunched up and headed toward them. Andrew stood motionless, his stomach pounding with fear. He was determined not to let Robin know how scared he was, and he doubled his fists into balls. He could get in a few hits, he thought, before the hounds jumped for his throat. They were coming fast, baying loudly, with their teeth showing and their red tongues flopping out. "Don't move," Robin said again.

Andrew couldn't have moved if he'd tried. He had never been so frightened in his life, and he thought if he ever got safely back it would be a miracle. The hounds were nearly at them now, their voices louder, and they looked gigantic. They stopped baying, and Andrew could see their gleaming eyes. They ran up, sniffing, circling the boys. One of them yipped, bounding around almost like a playful puppy. Fear made Andrew's eyes blur, then clear, and suddenly he realized they were wagging their tails!

"I was sure," Robin said. "They won't hurt people."

Andrew felt weak. "I'm glad you're right," he said.

He watched Robin get the leader by the collar, patting him and talking to him.

"Get that big one," Robin pointed. "Bring him this way. What we'll do is find them something really good to chase."

He led his hound rapidly through the water, scratching the dog's ears, coaxing him. The dog panted and leaped, happy to follow this new friend, while Andrew struggled behind with his. The third one milled cheerfully around, following the two boys' rapid progress away from Sally and Swampfire, and off at an angle from the path on which they had come.

Robin looked for deer signs. When he saw some young saplings that were stripped of leaves, he put his finger to his lips and crept forward. Luck was with them. Thirty yards farther on they found a deer. It was standing in the water not fifty feet ahead, and the dogs saw it too. Their tails rose up, their ears went forward, and when Robin and Andrew released them they were off and away so fast that both boys laughed.

"That was cool," Andrew said. "You really think fast."

Robin grinned. He gave Andrew a push. "I bet the warden'll have a fit—they'll never catch that deer. He'll lead them all day before they'll give up."

"That leaves us plenty of time to get back to the canoe," Andrew said. "Let's go get Sally. Hey, wait she was.

"There." Robin pointed.

The trees looked exactly alike and the water covered every landmark, but Robin seemed to have a compass in his head. They jogged back, and even more than handling the dogs, Andrew admired the way Robin found the right thicket, with Sally and Swampfire hidden inside.

"The dogs are gone," Robin said, and Andrew told her what had happened. She laughed, absently wiping some purple juice from her chin while she listened. The horse seemed huge standing there in the small space.

"I've been talking to him," Sally said. "He's getting tamer. He likes plums, too." Plums were all around in the thicket, growing on the trees, and Sally handed some to the boys.

"I've got rolls in my pocket," Andrew said, getting them out.

"I was wondering what those lumps were," Sally said. "We can make plum sandwiches."

"Not me. I want peanut butter."

"No, save that and the rolls too," Robin said. "We may need them later."

"But we won't," Andrew said. "This is lunch, and we'll be back at our camp by supper."

"We might not," Robin said.

"What's wrong?" Andrew said. "One of us can scout ahead and watch for the warden, and you said the dogs were gone for the day. We can't stay here."

"We can't go back, either," Robin said. "At least not that way. I've been thinking about it. . . . Even if we do get to the canoe, how would we put Swampfire in it?"

Sally and Andrew stood and looked at him. They had only thought of catching Swampfire, never of getting him home. Now they remembered the water lilies, and the beaver dam, and the impassable, high canal banks.

"Is there some other way to go?" Sally said.

Robin looked at the sky. "Yes. We could go to the lake. I've never been that far, but I can go by the sun and find it. From there it wouldn't be hard—my cabin's due southwest of it, and there's a path to Swamp Farm. That's the best way to get him home—" he jerked his head toward Swampfire—"and get around the warden too."

"And we have the compass, just in case." Sally was already excited at the thought.

But Andrew looked dubious. "Well, how hard is it? I mean, is Lake Drummond a big lake? Are you sure we can find it?"

"I'm sure," Robin said. "I've heard my pa say there's a lot of high ground around there, too."

"Oh, come on, Andrew," Sally broke in. "We've

88

got to. We can't lose Swampfire now."

"Shut up," Andrew said in a furious tone. He hated it when Sally made him feel little like that. "Of course I want to. It's just that, well . . ."

"Andrew," Sally said, "we've got to do it. The warden might shoot Swampfire."

They were right, Andrew thought. There really was no turning back. But all the same he knew how dangerous it might be, and he wished there were something else they could do. He put the rolls into the knapsack. "Okay," he said. "But we'd better be really careful."

"At least the men didn't see us," Sally said. "And they won't go back and tell Cousin Anne we're lost in the swamp." Then she realized what she had said. "We're not, are we? I mean, I bet you could find your way all over it, Robin."

"Most of it, I could," Robin said.

"We should get going, then," Andrew said. "Cousin Anne'll have a fit if we don't check in tomorrow. How long will it take us?"

"Probably three or four hours," Robin said. He was looking around, testing some sturdy maple branches. "Here. Help me break these."

They snapped them off, and Robin used his knife to slice points on the ends. They were like spears, sturdy and sharp, and as soon as Andrew held his he felt better.

89

"What do you think we'll need them for?" Sally said cheerfully. She was picking briars out of her hair and feeling full of energy.

"Probably nothing," Robin said. Andrew had a feeling he didn't want to scare them. "They'll be good for pushing aside vines, or as poles to test the water. Okay, that's sharp enough. Let's go."

They eased Swampfire back out of the thicket, careful not to scratch him, holding branches away from his slim legs. Then Robin led off with Sally and Swampfire in the middle and Andrew bringing up the rear. They felt more used to walking in the water now, and Robin was able to set a fast pace, with his pole to test the bottom. Swampfire came easily this time. He paced beside them, the rope slack. Sally thought again how wonderful he would be to ride. Some horses didn't care, but others enjoyed carrying you and going places, and she could tell he would be like that. It was the way he walked, with a quiet zest that seemed to spring from his heart. He seemed wild and free, as though the rope around his neck only held him because he let it, and Sally felt such a rush of affection for him she wanted to throw her arms around his neck. But she didn't want to frighten him, so she contented herself with reaching out and gently touching his glistening mane.

After thirty minutes Robin decided they had covered their tracks enough and he turned south, taking his direction from the sun. Now the ground rose, dark earth with giant trees whose smooth roots and boles stood out like great veins. The thick tree trunks were draped in vines and the sun streamed through in green-gold shafts high above their heads.

"Your father was right," Andrew said. "It is dry."

"He used to go all over," Robin said. "Before he got lame."

"It's like a church," Sally said, staring around.

The light did not penetrate far, and they walked in silence, their moccasins and Swampfire's hoofs making a thudding sound on the soft earth. "George Washington wanted to make this swamp a botanical garden," Andrew said.

"What happened?" Sally asked, climbing over a deadfall.

"I don't know. I guess he got too busy being president."

Soon they came to an old slough, a wide stream where the water looked deep. Robin eased his way down the bank to test it with his pole. He realized too late that the bank was slippery and with a scrambling splash, he fell in.

"Ohhh . . ." Sally ran forward.

Robin came up instantly, covered with green slime. He was smiling. "It's an otter slide," he said.

"Are you sure? I've never seen one." Andrew held out his pole and Robin grabbed it and climbed out.

"There're lots of otters in here," Robin said. "They love to play on these banks. I've seen five or six of them at once, sliding down. They go real fast."

"I've got to see one," Andrew said, starting to walk across on an old log. But he stopped so suddenly that Sally bumped into him, and then recoiled with horror. A snake lay in the center of the trunk, coiled in the sun, small head motionless, savage glass eyes watching them.

"Don't move," came Robin's low voice. They were frozen, feeling more horrified fascination than fear. The triangular head was still; only the tongue flickered and flickered, like drops of water in the sunlight.

Sally saw the body beginning to uncoil. "It's moving," she whispered, and felt her arms begin to tremble while the thing writhed and suddenly whipped its full length along the tree.

"Look out." Andrew was moving nervously back. "It's coming this . . ." and then the snake dropped into the water and was gone.

They sat down. The earth seemed dangerous, and the sun went under a cloud. Sally still trembled, and Robin came out and began to walk along the log.

"You'll never be as scared again," he said, "or the snake either." He smiled, and they managed to smile back.

"That was the biggest one I've ever seen!" Andrew said.

"It's like television." Sally was feeling pleased now the danger was over. "It's really like television."

"Snakes never stop growing until they die," Robin said. "And in here, they live a long time." He looked thoughtfully at Swampfire, who had seen the snake too. It was obvious that he hated them. His ears were back, he was pawing that ground and prancing in circles on his rope. "Now we'll never get him across the stream," Sally said.

"We've got to," Robin answered. "Take the end of the rope and go across."

Andrew looked doubtfully at the squishy ground beyond, but he started bravely across the tree trunk again. He felt his heart give a sickening lurch as one of his feet slipped. He thrashed wildly with his arms and managed to keep his balance, and reached the other side. "All set," he said.

"Pull him," Robin said.

But Swampfire wouldn't move, and Andrew's tugging did no good. Sally and Robin cajoled, they urged. "Get on the other side. Try pushing him."

But it didn't work. The horse still refused to go in the water, and finally Robin let go. He uprooted a small bush. He walked behind the great hindquarters, bunched and quivering. "Hang on when he jumps."

He whacked Swampfire across the rump with a sudden startling "whoosh" that sent the horse forward

93

in a tearing lunge, dragging away from Sally's grasp as though she were a flea. Swampfire careened into the water and swam across and tore up the opposite bank, until only Andrew, still holding the end of the rope and running behind, was finally able to stop him.

"Jeepers!" Andrew wiped his streaked and muddy face. They were all covered with mud, dripping, their feet like unreliable wobbly clods. Swampfire was shaking his head and whinnying. His ears were back, and Sally's heart sank. He would never like them now.

She got out one more piece of sugar from her carefully hoarded supply. "You have to trust us, Swampfire," she said. "We're trying to get you home." She held out the sugar, talking all the while in a low voice. "Then you can have sugar every day, and we'll ride you and play with you, and braid your mane too and make you beautiful again." Slowly his ears came up and he stopped circling around. "We can go anywhere we want, explore all the trails in the woods, have races. . . ." He was calming down. He sniffed at the sugar. Then he ate it. Sally reached up with her other hand and stroked his forehead.

"Try to get him going," Robin's voice broke in. "We have to keep moving." What he didn't say was that it was getting later in the afternoon. They still had plenty of daylight—Virginia twilights were long in June—but he didn't want to slow down.

Sally took the rope and tugged gently, and they started forward again.

"Wow," said Andrew. "I thought we were really going to lose him that time."

"You held on, though," Robin said. "That was good."

Now Robin and Andrew walked in front together, with their spears. Every now and then Robin looked at Andrew's compass, but mostly he used the sun as a guide. He kept the pace steady, and they got into a kind of rhythm. They waded pools, they slogged through mud, they speeded up at places where the ground was firm. They walked with the scent of magnolia and jasmine in their noses, and for the first time they saw Spanish moss hanging from the trees.

Sally never got tired of watching Robin choose the best way to go. It seemed as easy for him as breathing. Sometimes he would come to a standstill, then turn in a slow circle, marking the birds' nests and the wind's direction. Then, somehow sure of his bearings, he would start on again. When he came to a place where the ground looked smooth he would say, "Bog. Put your feet where I do." She and Andrew and Swampfire would follow carefully, while Robin chose a way safely around it.

Andrew thought that what he liked best was the silence. At home there were always cars whizzing by, or planes flying over, and roars from trucks. There were whistles and toots, doors slamming, and crashing sounds in every city block. Out here it seemed so quiet that Andrew's thoughts sounded like someone talking to him. There were sounds, but not the kind that bothered you. It was almost possible to hear things flying, crawling, growing, and blooming. And like themselves, walking. Slowly the swamp was beginning to be a part of them, or they of it. No wonder Robin knew so much about it, Andrew thought. If you lived in here long enough, it would be like knowing about your own self.

Finally Robin stopped at the base of a tall pine tree. "I think we're near the lake," he said. "The ground is rising and I saw an osprey. Let's go up and see."

He swung himself up and they followed, going up the close-set branches like rungs in a ladder. At the top Robin pointed. "There it is!" he said. Sally and Andrew could see flying crows and a rising mist. Then they saw glistening water, with reeds gently moving in the wave wash at its edge. Sally squinted, trying to see how big it was.

"Look at the sunset," Andrew said. It was lovely, full of deep pink stripes, but the sun itself was nearly gone.

"It's later than I thought," Robin said. "The lake's not so far, but I can't find my cabin without the sun. We can't get there tonight."

"Not tonight?" Sally suddenly felt funny. "What'll we do?"

"Camp," Andrew said. "What else? That's what you've always wanted." She knew he was mad that this had happened, and he was taking it out on her, but that didn't make her feel any better.

Robin had started down the tree, but he stopped so suddenly that Sally almost stepped on his head. He was listening. "Shhh."

They all heard a sound as though something were moving in the bushes. Swampfire snorted, ears pricked. He pawed impatiently, and Robin looked at him.

"He's fretting," he whispered, "but I can't tell what it is."

The sound stopped, and they slid lower. It started again. Something was circling Swampfire, and their tree. Goose bumps went up Sally's neck. She could feel danger all over her skin.

"It's an animal," Robin whispered. "Scare it off."

Their spears were propped against the bottom of the tree. They jumped the rest of the way down and grabbed them. Robin beat his spear against the bushes and Andrew and Sally copied him. They ran in a circle, beating and yelling, and then in a bigger one, and then they stopped to listen. All they heard was the late afternoon breeze, high in the trees.

"It's gone," Robin said.

Sally felt a chill of fear. She wished Delilah were there. An owl called, so close to them and so loud it made them all jump. The setting sun seemed to have come to the dark wall of the trees and stopped, as though the world of living things ended at the edge of the swamp, not daring to go farther. They were alone, with the great cypress, the vines, with the black water, and dark silence. Even the birds were still. Sally shivered, all of a sudden feeling terribly afraid.

Maybe Andrew was right, she thought. We should have listened to him this morning. She went back to Swampfire and untied his rope, and she saw her hands shaking.

"Oh, Swampfire," she whispered. "We never should have come so far. I wonder if we'll ever see the daylight again."

7

"WE'VE GOT to build a platform to sleep on," Robin was saying, "in a protected place." He turned to Sally. "You stay here with Swampfire while we find it."

She nodded dumbly, trying to fight down her fears. She tried to tell herself that an Indian girl wouldn't be afraid, or even if she were, she would be brave anyway. But it didn't work. Whatever had circled them had been big, and it was real. Sally couldn't help thinking of monsters, the kind she had seen on television. She knew those were plastic, with ketchup for blood and men inside them. Still, it was a scary thought, and in spite of herself she imagined huge creatures jumping out, white-green eyes glowing. She felt her stomach flop over, and she put her hand on Swampfire's neck.

"You're not scared, are you?" Sally whispered.

He blew his nostrils at her, swishing his tail at the gnats, and she relaxed a little. The red-gold hairs on his neck stood out in the last of the sunlight, over-lapping one another tightly on his skin. She loved the way his silver forelock spilled down, so long it separated over the sides of his head. It almost cov-ered the deep hollows in front of his ears, and he looked so beautiful she began to feel better. Fright-ened or not, he was worth it. And this *was* the only way they had to get him home. On a sudden impulse she leaned against him, and the horse was startled and leaped away.

"You're scaring him," Sally heard Andrew's voice. He had come back without her knowing.

"No I'm not," she said, feeling silly.

"Robin's found a good place," Andrew said. "Come on."

She followed, embarrassed that he had seen how she felt. She pretended she had to straighten out a knot in the rope, and by the time she finished they had come to the campsite.

It was in a grove of cedars, next to a big fallen log. It made a good place for a fire, because the trees grew in sandy soil, and the smoke mixed with the strong scent of cedar would keep away mosquitoes. Robin had already laid one—a crisscross of logs over a pile of chunky peat moss for kindling. Now he was cutting saplings for the platform, and Sally looped Swampfire's rope around a bush so he could graze, and helped the boys drive long forked poles in the ground in a rectangle.

They cut two more long poles to make the sides of the platform. Then they gathered heavy vines and strung them back and forth across the frame, and branches to weave with the vines for a mattress. Robin showed them how to tie bunches of twigs, points down, on each leg of the platform for snake guards. Cedar trees were too prickly for snakes to climb on, so there was no danger from above.

"There," Andrew said. He tied a last vine around the bunch of twigs he held, and stood up. "That should do it. No snake could get above that."

"It's getting hard to see," Sally said.

"We'll light the fire," said Robin. The dry peat caught quickly, and Sally was relieved that it looked so bright.

"We may have a problem about food," Andrew said. "We've only got the rolls and peanut butter."

"And Instant Breakfast," Sally said. "That's like a whole meal."

"If you're on a diet, that is," Andrew said. He was beginning to feel very hungry, and it was making him irritable.

"There're blackberries all around us," Robin said. "And wild cabbages. They're not so bad and they'll fill us up. I'll see what I can find." He disappeared in the dark, and Andrew looked around for something to do.

"We need water," he said to Sally. "I saw a stream when I went back for you. I'll go get some." He dug the pail out of the pack and opened it up, and switched on the flashlight.

"Okay," Sally said. "I'll get Swampfire fixed up."

Andrew walked into the darkness and Sally untangled Swampfire's rope and moved him closer into the firelight. The horse's coat was streaked, his mane was matted, his tail hung in straggles, tangled with burrs and leaves and sticks. She hardly knew where to begin, but she started by picking the burrs out of his mane. While she worked she wondered what it would have been like to have been an Indian girl living in here a long time ago. She wondered if she would have been afraid of the dark then, too, and decided she probably wouldn't. Indians were used to it. She and her mother and father and Andrew would have had a tepee and they would all have been wearing skin clothes, and moccasins, the real kind, not the kind people tried to copy now.

Sally had seen Andrew square his shoulders to go into the trees, even though he had a flashlight. Indians certainly didn't have any flashlights. They wouldn't even have known what they were. But if that snake this afternoon had bitten her or Andrew, her Indian parents would have known exactly what to do. They would have used herbs, and all their knowledge of woodcraft. There weren't any hospitals then; Indians had to count on their own abilities. She wondered if all their lore was written down. She hoped so—it shouldn't be forgotten. People weren't always near a town or hospital, even now.

She finished Swampfire's mane and decided not to groom his tail. He might not like it, although so far he had shown no inclination to kick. She led him to a tree at the edge of the clearing, wishing the boys wouldn't take so long. Andrew, at least, should be back by now.

But Andrew was concentrating on finding the stream. He was flattered that Robin was treating him like an equal, and he was determined not to let himself be afraid. He was aware of the branches, twisted and grotesque in the dim light, but he kept his eyes on the flashlight's beam and tried not to look around. Even so, he felt how black it was and how spooky the vines looked draped over the black trees, like tentacles waiting to grab him.

When he reached the stream crickets were chirping loudly in the grass, and he stooped down to fill the pail. Then he jerked upright. Something was skittering off a branch, not ten feet away. It dropped into the water with a splash that made Andrew's blood run cold. He tried to see which way it went and for a minute, thinking of something appearing suddenly at his feet and running up his legs, he had to fight a wild impulse to turn and run. Back to the meadow, back to the warden, back to anywhere away from here.

But nothing came, and finally Andrew moved one foot. Nothing jumped at him. He moved the other, and still he was all right. When his heartbeats calmed down he dipped the pail. The water bubbled in and he lifted it up. He started back toward the camp, going faster, rushing ahead of his fear. He almost ran into the firelight.

"Hi," Sally said.

"Hi. Is Robin back?"

She shook her head, and Andrew set the pail down. "Here's the water. I was scared."

She wanted to say she was too, but she couldn't because it might have made it come back again, so she just nodded. "I'll put the water on to boil," she said.

"Why?"

"That's what people always do when they're camping," Sally said. "Give it here."

But it was not so easy. They put the pail on the fire, and the flames started to go out. They tried putting it on a flat stone at the side of the fire, but it wouldn't get hot. Then they thought of two forked sticks in the ground with the pail hanging from a long stick in between. The water began to boil just

as Robin came back, his knapsack full of blackberries. He was carrying six small cabbages.

"Two apiece," he said proudly. "They're tender,
they'll cook fast." He dropped them in the boiling
pot, and Sally and Andrew smiled. "It worked."

"What?"

"The pot. We didn't know if it was right."

"Oh." Robin grinned. "It'd better be. I'm hungry."

While the cabbages cooked, they worked on their
camp, getting more firewood, clearing off the sand.
Then they sat down and ate. The cabbages were good.
They tasted a little bit like broccoli, and the blackberries were big and juicy. Sally used twigs to dig
globs of peanut butter out of the jar, and spread it on
the rolls. She handed them around, and everyone
washed his food down with sips of the cooking
water. Andrew pointed out that it was like eating
salad and meat. "Protein and green, protein and
green," he said. He said it in just the tone of one of
their aunts, who was a bug on health food, and Sally
could tell that he wasn't upset any more about coming this far into the swamp.

Afterward they lay with their backs propped
against the log and, watching the fire, listened to a
chorus of owls. Swampfire stood very near, his rope
looped over a branch. He was calm and majestic,
every now and then cocking his ears at the blackness
around them. Insects droned everywhere, and the

stars were buried deep in a hot, black sky. Heat light-ning flickered far to the east.

"You know," Andrew said, "everybody used to live like this, just in the woods with campfires."

"Umn," Sally murmured. She was getting sleepy. "If you had been a person then, and somebody told you about cars and planes, it would've really sounded queer."

Andrew turned over and scratched his knee. "I like this better. If we lived this way all the time, we'd really know how."

Robin got up and circled the fire. "You wouldn't like it in the winter," he said. Then he stretched out on the platform and yawned. "I wonder what the warden is doing," he said.

"He's probably mad," Andrew said.

"Are you sure he didn't see you?" Robin said.

Andrew grinned. "You asked me that before. Yes, I'm sure." But he realized Robin was worried, and he added, "Even if he does find out it's us later, Cousin Anne will help us." At least, Andrew thought, I hope so.

Sally was beginning to feel fear pushing at her again, somewhere inside. She got up so she wouldn't feel it, and got on the platform. "What're we doing about keeping watch?" she said.

"We'll take turns," Robin said. "The main thing is to keep the fire built up."

"I'll start," Andrew said. "I'll wake you up next."

"Okay, but don't take too long a turn," Robin said. "You might fall asleep."

"I won't."

Sally's eyes were already closing. They had been awake half the night before and walked a long way today, and in spite of her fear she was too tired to stay awake. Robin had no trouble dozing off either. Andrew sat up very straight to keep himself alert. He planned to list the birds he had seen, and make notes for his science notebook. But after a while he began to have difficulty keeping his eyes open. He got up several times and put more moss and peat on the fire, and still drowsiness kept coming over him. Finally he woke Robin.

"It hasn't been very long," he said, "but I can't help it. I can't stay awake."

Robin pushed himself up. "That's okay," he said. "I'll do it."

Andrew fell asleep immediately, and Robin looked at Sally. She was sleeping soundly, and he wondered if he would ever get her awake when her turn came. Then he checked the fire and stared into it, thinking. He wished he knew what that animal had been. He thought it was a big bobcat, but he wished he could be sure. Still, there hadn't been any more signs of it; he had been half listening all the while they were making camp, and he hadn't heard anything. Swampfire hadn't seemed uneasy either, and now he was dozing, his ears half-back and his eyes half-closed, standing on three legs. Robin threw more wood on the fire, building it as big as he could.

He thought about Sally. He liked the way she talked, so fast and always wanting to do everything. He liked her hair, too. It was a good color. He wondered what she thought of him. He knew Andrew liked him, and he was pretty sure Sally did too, but he didn't know as much about girls.

Robin liked them more than any people he had ever known. He liked the way they noticed everything and wanted to learn how to do it. He thought of them in school, talking to their friends. He wished he could be like that. Not living in the city—he wouldn't want that. But the way they spoke their feelings out. He hoped he could learn to talk like they did, in here where he felt his strongest self. But so far he couldn't; he was still the same.

Then he shrugged. There was still some time to go. He began to think about the best route home, and he realized he was yawning. He probably should wake Sally up. But he started thinking again, this time about the warden, and the next time he yawned, he didn't know it. He had fallen asleep.

Two hours went by. The fire died lower and lower. The camp was still, though far from quiet. "Pond-toes," or swamp rabbits, called their strange mink-like snarls nearby. Far off a huge tree, standing for fifty years, picked this night to fall—a slow and rumbling sound that quivered through the swamp like thunder. Crickets and the locusts droned their loud and rhythmic calls, drowning out the children's deep and regular breathing. Even Swampfire slept, his head low.

But then the big horse began to stir uneasily. His eyes opened at a noise so slight it was hardly noticeable. His ears cocked, as he heard the bushes begin to rustle. He snorted.

Robin heard him, and woke up. The fire was very low, almost out. A feeling ran across the back of Robin's neck, prickling his skin in an ancient warning. Something was walking around their campsite, gently cracking twigs and pushing aside the thickets. It sounded like an animal, a big one.

Robin shook Andrew and Sally. "Get up," he whispered. "Help me get wood on the fire." He was already grabbing at branches in their platform, sliding off and throwing them in the glowing coals. But the fire was too low. The wood wouldn't catch.

"Where're the matches?"

No one could find them. Andrew ran to look in the knapsack. Sally switched on the flashlight. Now the clearing lit up a little and they strained to see along the black corridors of the trees. The noise stopped, but still they had an awful sense of something out there, coming closer.

"Hurry," Robin said in a low voice, swerving off to one side. "Spread out."

Andrew moved to the opposite side. Sally felt terror grab her, make her ache, but she did as he said, clutching her spear, staring at the trees. They could hear branches shaking, then break. Swampfire whinnied, the sudden sound shocking the woods into silence. Seconds ticked by, and then the children heard grunts. They were louder and nearer. Andrew and Sally backed up to the big fallen log, tensing as the bushes shook and waved. The branches parted before a massive head. The body pushed out, and they saw a huge black bear.

They saw his red eyes, his flat, wedged skull, his ivory teeth. They could see his great form rise up, forepaws looking as big as tennis rackets, straining wide from his huge forearms and shoulders. They could even see the tips of his claws, long and stained and curved. The bear lumbered forward and came down again, swaying at the edge of the clearing. He made a sort of howling grunt, and Sally felt her knees shaking. Swampfire reared, pawing the air. His rope was taut, straining on his neck. Again he whinnied, and this time it was a peal of rage.

Andrew was closest. He saw the horse—trapped— saw them all, standing still. His brain felt hot. There was no time for him to plan, for the bear was moving toward Swampfire. Andrew ran to untie the rope, but his fingers fumbled. He couldn't undo it.

Robin threw his spear. All his weight was behind the stroke as the spear went into the bear's shoulder. The bear grunted and turned. His forepaw came across and slapped the shaft. It broke like a match stick and fell out.

Then Sally was there too, sending her spear hard at the bear's flank, making him turn. Robin ran to the bear's other side, waving the knapsack, yelling. The bear seemed confused. He swayed from side to side. Sally had only the flashlight, so she waved that. She ran backward, tripped, and fell. The flashlight flickered and went out. The bear took a step toward her and Robin swung up on a tree branch, whistling, yelling, distracting the animal from the fallen girl. The bear half rose on his hind legs again, blinking and peering around.

Andrew saw one of the long branches in the fire. Its tip had finally caught, and he grabbed it. There was no time to aim. He ran with the torch straight for the bear's head. It caught the bear in the nose and he turned, half rising, flailing the air. As Andrew scuttled backward, the bear's claws caught him with a swipe, but Andrew dodged out of reach. The animal put his nose down and pawed at it, while Sally scrambled up and Robin pulled her into the tree.

Then the bear stood up, waving his paws.

"Can he climb?" Sally whispered to Robin.

"I don't know," Robin said.

It seemed like forever, but it was only a few seconds that he stood there while they tried not to move. Finally, when they thought they couldn't hold on any longer, he came down on all fours again. Then, like a big black shadow, swaying and growling, he lumbered away.

For a long time no one spoke. No one even breathed. All they could hear were their pounding hearts, until a nightingale called nearby and they realized the bear was really gone. They jumped down, and relief made everyone talk at once, as they clustered around Swampfire.

"Did you see those teeth?"

"Yes. I thought he was going to charge when he stood up."

"He was just trying to see better," Robin said. "They don't have very good eyesight."

Sally giggled. "He probably didn't know what to make of us. He probably thought we were crazy."

"We probably scared him to death," Andrew said, feeling bolder now the bear was gone.

"He scared me to death," Sally said. "Andrew! Look at your arm!"

They looked at the long scratches, like grooves. "It's lucky you weren't any closer when he hit you," Robin said. He picked up the flashlight and shined it closely on Andrew's skin.

"I never even felt it," Andrew said, feeling pleased.

Robin sponged off Andrew's arm with the cooking water, which was clean because it had been boiled. Then he found some large round leaves at the edge of the clearing.

"Do you think he was after Swampfire, or us?" Andrew said.

"Probably neither. He smelled us, and came to see if he could get anything to eat." Robin was laying the leaves on Andrew's arm. Sally watched carefully to see what he did. "We'll just keep washing it out and it'll be fine. There won't be any scar or anything."

"Oh." Andrew was disappointed. He could think of nothing better than having a bear scar. "Do you think he'll come back?"

"Not if we keep the fire built up," Robin said. "Those cedar logs went down too fast. We've got to use more peat, it keeps a better flame."

They found the matches on the ground near the knapsack, and collected more peat and took care of the fire. Sally untied Swampfire and led him around the clearing, talking to him and giving him the last of the water. Finally the horse stopped snorting and watching the trees, so she tied him up again, and they crawled on what was left of the platform, their spears by their sides. It was a new feeling to have driven away a bear in the middle of the night, and Andrew thought he liked it.

"Now it'll be hard to get to sleep," he said.

But for some reason it wasn't. They saw the moon setting in a big white ring, which Robin said meant the weather was going to change.

"What makes it?" Sally said.

"I don't know."

And shortly afterward they began to doze, and soon, in spite of Andrew's prediction, they fell once more into a deep, untroubled sleep.

8

THE DAY CAME gold and green, flashing them awake like the wings of the birds that streaked the sky with light and color. Sally opened her eyes and saw two chipmunks chattering in a tree over her head. She turned her head and saw Robin throwing wet sand on the fire to put the last of it out.

"Hi," he said.

"Hi."

"I didn't want any of the smoke to show in the day-light, in case someone's looking," Robin said.

Sally sat up, remembering. The warden. Swamp-fire. The bear. It seemed like a dream, and she could hardly believe it had really happened. But it had. . . . There were the scratches on Andrew's arm, outflung in sleep, to prove it. They looked better, all scabbed over, but still she shivered, thinking of the bear's big claws.

Swampfire was standing by the trees, beams of sunlight dappling his sleek flanks. Sally jumped up and rummaged for the last of the sugar. He whickered when he saw her coming, but when she stretched out her palm, Robin heard her gasp.

"Robin, look!" she said. "Oh, you poor thing!"

Where Swampfire had reared and pulled on the rope he had rubbed raw places on his neck. They were crusted with dried blood.

"We never noticed last night," Sally said. "That's terrible!"

Andrew had waked up, yawning. "We can't use that rope around his neck any more," he said. "We need a halter."

"I know," Robin said. He got more leaves, the kind he had used on Andrew's arm, and sponged Swampfire's neck. Then he caught hold of a grapevine. "We can make one out of this. If we braid it, it'll lie flat."

Sally helped him pull it off the tree, and Andrew stripped the leaves. It was hard to remember how a halter went, but they figured it out by standing near Swampfire and looking at his head as they braided the vines and tied the sections together.

"There." Andrew finished a final knot.

"I'll hold him," Sally said, patting Swampfire's nose. "He may not like it."

But Swampfire didn't seem to mind. He lowered his head when Robin slid the halter up over his ears and tied the chin strap. There was only one loose place, and after that was fixed Sally tied the rope to the nose band and tugged gently. Instantly the horse stepped forward, and Andrew looked pleased.

"He likes it!" he said. "Now he won't choke himself."

"Or run away," Sally said.

"He's getting easier with us," Robin said. "I don't think he would."

"I wonder if he'd let us ride him." Sally hitched up her shorts. "I know how. I took lessons."

"He might," Robin said. "But this isn't a very good place to start. We better wait." He picked up the tin plates from last night and put them in the knapsack. The sight reminded Andrew of food. He got the Instant Breakfast powder and mixed it with water. "Gross," he sputtered. "This stuff tastes horrible!"

"You're supposed to use milk," Sally said. "Drink it anyway, we need our strength." She knew she sounded exactly like their mother, but she was beginning to see why grown-ups said these things. Some of them were true.

"We could hunt for turtle eggs." Robin pointed to some long drags in the wet sand. "That's where they lay them. They make good eating."

"Ooh, no," Sally said, thinking that if the eggs weren't fresh, inside would be crawling baby turtles.

Robin grinned. "Okay, then we'd better start. I

heard the dogs again before you woke up. They were a long way off, but still, it's better to keep moving. Sweep our tracks away while I climb the tree."

Sally and Andrew used branches to get the sand as smooth as possible. "How mad do you think Cousin Anne'll be, if we're late getting back?" Sally said.

"I hope not mad enough to make us give Swamp-fire back," Andrew said.

"Give him back to who?" Sally said.

"I don't know, but he must have come from somewhere," Andrew said.

"Umnn." Sally didn't want to think about that. She threw her broom in the bushes and watched Robin shinny down the tree. He shouldered into the knapsack. "Nothing in sight," he said. "But the lake is really clear. It's not far at all."

They left the camp and walked through the cedar grove, feeling a little sorry to leave their own private camp that they had built and defended.

"Do you think we could ever find this place again?" Sally said.

"I think so," Robin said.

"I'll remember it, every time I fight some guy at school," Andrew said. "I'll remember that I scared a bear." He raised his arms over his head, bowing to an imaginary crowd. He looked funny, and Sally laughed.

Out of the cedar trees the day was already hot, and

the sandy soil changed to greenish mud, glistening in the sunshine. It was dotted with bushes and patches of reeds, and Robin's gaze swept over it. Dozens of white herons stood motionless all through the reeds. The ones nearby flew off a way, startled at the sight of humans, and settled back again.

"Oh, beautiful," Andrew breathed. Every time they surprised an animal or bird he felt as though he had looked through a window into a huge wild room where it was lonely and wonderful to be, all at the same time. The one thing that was missing was people, and he was curiously glad. You felt alone but you felt good, all at the same time. Andrew wondered how that could be, but forgot it when Robin startled him out of his daydream. "Come on," Robin said, and Andrew hurried to catch up.

Robin took Swampfire's rope, and picked a place to try the mud, but after four steps he sank in up to his ankles. Swampfire reared, pulling back to firmer ground. Robin led him to one side and then started forward again, but again the horse came to a full halt, feet firmly planted.

"It's not safe—" Robin squinted at the mud—"and he knows it. It must be quicksand."

Sally and Andrew stared at the innocent looking mud, and Andrew picked up a piece of wood and threw it. It landed silently and sank in quickly, but not before they heard a sort of sucking sound. When it was gone nothing showed on the surface at all, not even a bubble, and Sally shuddered.

"Good thing Swampfire's with us," was all Andrew said, but he looked pale under his tan.

They went a hundred yards to the right, and then another, and finally there was a firmer, grassy stretch. This time Swampfire went willingly. They gave him plenty of rope, and he walked ahead through low bushes, then farther along on patches of sugarcane. He walked on anything that had roots, instinctively knowing the roots made the mud firm. The children followed carefully, stepping like cats on a flat stone here, a half-buried log there, a patch of tarmac farther on. Sweat poured down their faces; the sun was broiling hot. Swampfire's mane flopped on his neck as he walked, head down, ears forward, sniffing and testing every step.

The mud finally gave way to grassland, up a little hill. The grass gave way to trees, and the trees opened up on a small, sandy beach. Mourning doves "hooed" in the branches. Vines hung cool into the clear, brown water. They had reached the lake.

It looked untouched, sitting peacefully in what seemed the middle of nowhere, and it was much larger than they had expected, almost a mile across.

"Do many people know about it?" Sally asked.

"Not many," Robin said. "Some men used to come in hunting season, I think, before they made it government land around here."

"It's really a crater," Andrew said. "I read about it in a book at Cousin Anne's. It's the highest land in the swamp."

Swampfire waded in, plunging his muzzle down, snorting and blowing. He lifted his head and looked around, water streaming from his muzzle. Suddenly he began to crumple, and Sally shrieked, "He's falling!"

Robin laughed. "No, he's not, he's just going to roll."

They watched him heave around in the water, kicking his legs in the air. Back and forth he went on his back, making a wild thrashing. It gave them all the same idea at once.

"Let's go swimming," Robin said.

"Is it safe?" Sally asked.

"What about the bottom?" Andrew put one foot in it.

"It's sand," Robin said. "And if there were any snakes Swampfire's scared them away."

Robin went in first, splashing the water with his hands. He walked out till the water was up to his waist. He cupped his hands in the cool, brown surface and lifted them to drink, and then poured the rest of the water over his head and face. He was grinning. "It feels good," he said. Then he flung himself backward and swam wildly along the beach, and they rushed in too.

The water was soft, and it slid over their hair like silk. They went under and stood up and went under again, cooling every inch of their hot skins. Sally stayed near Swampfire, secretly thinking that if a snake came, she could always climb on his back. Eventually he splashed his way out and she followed, aimlessly letting him graze in the trees. Her mind was wandering, so at first she didn't notice the boat drifting along the shoreline farther down the lake. Then she came to.

"The warden!" she yelped. "Isn't that him?"

The boys sank without a sound. Only the tops of their heads showed, slick and shiny like two otters sneaking ashore. They wormed their way across the beach on their stomachs, and eased into the trees beside Sally and Swampfire.

"How did he get here?"

Robin squinted out through the trees. "The canal must be open all the way to the lake," he said.

"What'll we do now?" Andrew asked.

"Maybe he'll go away," Sally said. "I don't see any dogs."

"I bet he left them behind this time," Robin said, and Andrew laughed.

"You know," said Sally, "if this were a movie, we'd have known he was going to be there. They'd have played scary music first, and then you'd have seen him, in a close-up, looking mean."

"Yeah," Andrew said, "smiling, about to eat the children."

"I saw a movie once," Robin said.

Andrew and Sally felt embarrassed; they didn't know what to say because they had seen so many. "What was it?" Sally asked.

"It was about fighting with airplanes," Robin said. "I liked it."

"That kind is exciting," Sally said.

The boat was coming closer, and now they could hear its engine. They shrank back as it got near. The warden and two men were in it. It came on until it turned in toward them and then it landed not twenty yards to their right along the lake shore. The men got out. They were wearing hip boots, and they clomped ashore through the trees, their voices just loud enough for the children to hear. "We'd better put in a call to Norfolk for the helicopter if we don't . . ." Their voices trailed off as they disappeared.

"Where're they going?" Sally whispered.

"Might be their camp's in there," Robin said.

"I hope it's a long way in," Andrew said.

Five minutes went by, and then five minutes more. Robin studied the lake shore. Except for this little beach, it seemed a solid mass of tangled trees. He squinted at the sun. "My cabin's there." He pointed across to the southwest. "But I don't know how we're going to get there. All this shore is too thick to walk through, or else it'll be more quicksand. And the warden's back in there somewhere, besides."

"All we need to get across the lake is a boat like the warden's," Sally said.

"Why don't we just borrow his?" Andrew said.

They looked at each other. "That's the kind of thing grown people don't like," Sally said.

"I know, but we can give it a shove when we're over there. It'll probably drift back by itself," Andrew said.

"What about Swampfire?" Sally said.

"He can swim. We'll lead him," Andrew answered. "There isn't any other way. Come on." He stood up.

But Sally didn't move. She had been getting more and more worried about how Cousin Anne would feel about all the things they were doing. If Cousin Anne were really mad at them she might, indeed, make them get rid of Swampfire. Or even worse, hand him over to the warden. Sally looked at Robin. "What do you think?"

"Wait here a minute," he answered. He left them to scout the beach, and came back to report it was clear. "I think we can do it," he said. "We do need a boat. And we're not stealing. We're only getting Swampfire home."

Sally couldn't argue about that, so she followed the boys and led Swampfire out on the beach.

The warden's boat was a flat-bottomed fiberglass with a powerful looking engine. It had a specially built big propeller on a short shaft, designed for high speeds in shallow water. In the bottom were large oars, which Andrew and Robin put in the oarlocks. They didn't dare use the engine because of the noise, and anyway they didn't know how to run it.

Andrew and Sally got in and pushed off while Robin led Swampfire into the water. He came willingly, and Robin started swimming. Robin reached the boat and held onto its side, pulling Swampfire's rope until the horse was swimming too. He took great strokes, kicking out with his front feet, heading straight for the boat. Robin let go its edge and swam to the side, while Sally and Andrew rowed frantically to get out of Swampfire's way.

"My gosh," Andrew muttered. "This isn't going to work. He's trying to climb in the boat!"

For a minute it was touch and go, but Robin swam backward, pulling Swampfire away just in time. Then he worked his way gradually along the rope to Swampfire's side.

"What's he doing?" Sally said.

"He's going to get on him," Andrew said.

There was a confused minute when Sally and Andrew could see the water churning and Swampfire swimming in a circle. Then the horse seemed to settle down, and they saw the boy on his back.

"Go on," Robin called. "I think he'll follow you."

They speeded up, and the horse fell back slightly. But he kept coming, and they saw Robin patting his neck. "He's doing fine," the boy called softly. "Keep going, people can see us."

"He's right. Watch the place the warden went ashore," Andrew panted at Sally. She nodded, working too hard to speak. Rowing this fast was much harder than she remembered rowing in a city park. They were well out in the lake by now, but so far all they had seen back on the shore were three crows, flying low across the water.

In ten minutes they had passed the middle. Swampfire swam easily, his head high, following ten yards behind the boat. It was almost as though carrying Robin had steadied him for this long swim. Robin looked as though he were enjoying himself and for a minute Sally envied him, wondering if she would have the nerve to change places. Then Andrew said he could see bottom, and they had to watch where they were going. The southern shoreline was coming closer, with big cypress trees standing in the water like people walking to meet them. An osprey flew by, fishing. Andrew and Sally looked for a beach. They saw some gray sand and rowed toward it.

"Hurry," came Robin's voice. "They're back there."

They heard a distant shout and turned around. Three tiny figures were moving around on the shore they had left, barely visible in the distance.

"Oh, boy," Andrew said. "We've had it."

"Duck down," Sally said. "We're so far away now they might not be able to see us. Maybe they'll think the boat just drifted loose."

"Fat chance," Andrew said, but he ducked down anyway, and rowed harder. Robin was lying flat along Swampfire's neck, half under water. Swampfire started rising out of the water. His feet touched bottom before the boat scraped across a layer of leaves. He plunged out onto the sand, the water showering up from his legs. Robin slid from his back just as he gave a mighty shake to get the water from his mane and tail. Quickly Robin led him out of sight into the thickets.

Sally and Andrew jumped out of the boat and crouched beside it. "Maybe we shouldn't shove it off," Andrew said. "The warden's seen us, anyway."

Sally nodded. "That's what I told you. It's a valuable boat. He'll be twice as mad if it's drifting."

They crouched low and dragged it up on the beach, and tied its bow line to a heavy log. They ran in the bushes after Robin, who was already slogging west through mud and green scum.

"You know what?" Andrew said. "Now they've seen Swampfire, with us."

"I don't think they could see us well enough to know us," Robin said, but his voice didn't sound very positive.

"Does the warden know where your cabin is?" Sally asked. And then she remembered he did. "Let's go faster," she said.

"We'll only stay there long enough to eat," Robin said. "That is, if you want to." He seemed suddenly shy.

"Sure," Andrew said. "I'm starving."

"We don't have much . . ." Robin sounded hesitant.

"We'd love to come," Sally said firmly. She put her hair behind her ears and thought about seeing Robin's cabin. He seemed to belong more in the swamp than connected to parents. She hoped she liked them. If they were queer, it would ruin everything.

They hurried ahead, hungry and hot again, now they were away from the lake. In fifteen minutes they came out onto a path which led to a stretch of open meadow where they found themselves in clouds of wildflowers. They went through scrub trees growing in sandy soil, and while they were walking they smelled smoke. Robin frowned.

"It's my pa," he said. "He must have lit the fire himself because I wasn't there to do it."

Sally wondered why he would mind his father lighting a fire without him and then she remembered Cousin Anne's words . . . "Father's all crippled with arthritis, hardly gets around."

Robin was hurrying on, over planks in a marsh.

They came out of the woods at a cleared field, and on the other side a cabin with a porch stood under two big oak trees. It looked deserted until a big white hound ran out barking at Swampfire, but Robin called to him and he stopped.

"This is Ghoster," Robin said. The big dog jumped around, licking Robin's face and whining.

"He's great," Andrew said. "Why didn't you bring him before?"

"You wanted to see the animals," Robin said. "He scares them off."

Robin tied Swampfire to the rail around a small lot that held a cow, and led them inside. His father was sitting in a chair with chunks of wood in his lap. Sally and Andrew could see that he had once been a tall and strong man, but now his arms and feet were twisted and lumpy. He held his back stiffly, but his smile was warm.

"Welcome," he said. "You're just in time. I was just trying to get this dratted fire goin' to start dinner."

"I'll do it, Pa," Robin said. "We brought a horse, Pa."

"Well, now, how 'bout that. Good one?"

Robin nodded. "We like him a lot."

"Want to keep him here?"

What a perfect grown-up, Sally thought. Imagine not asking where Swampfire came from, or right away telling the reasons why it wouldn't work out.

"I don't know yet," Robin said.

His father nodded. "Well, go say hello to your ma while I get acquainted with your friends. She's lying down in back."

Robin went through a back door and Andrew took the chunks of wood from the man's bent arms. "I'll build the fire," he said.

Sally went out to see about Swampfire. Ghoster was sniffing at the horse's heels, and Swampfire looked as though he might kick. She whistled gently and the hound trotted over. He stood in front of her, waving his tail. "You're a nice dog," Sally said.

He licked her hand, and then he cocked his ears because Robin was coming out of the cabin doorway.

"The smoke!" he said. "The smoke we smelled walking here. Pa hadn't started the fire yet, so it's coming from somewhere else." He looked all around the clearing, and then above the tops of the trees.

"But where could it be from?" Sally said.

"I don't know," Robin said. He started walking across the yard. "But we'd better find out."

9

THEY RAN OUT into the clearing, over the marsh planks and back to the scrub trees. Already the smoke smelled stronger. Andrew caught up with them, and they followed their noses until they came around a thicket and saw a thin ribbon of smoke curling up ahead.

"Duck." Robin jumped behind some bushes. "It could be a campfire. If it is, the people are somewhere around."

But after they watched a little more, they saw the smoke was spiraling up in two places.

"I can't see the fire," Sally said.

"There're three of them!" Andrew pointed to another spiral, farther along in the wild flowers.

"There's a fourth!" Sally stood up, shading her eyes against the sun. It was hard to see clearly in the glare,

Robin went cautiously to the first one. Standing right above it, he could see the fire itself for the first time. It was deep in the peat. He poked hard with a big branch, trying to put it out. He got the top part, but there was still more lower down, and it seemed to be spreading underground. It was much more serious than it had looked at first, and finally Robin stopped digging.

"How do you think it started?" Sally said.

"Lightning, probably," Robin said. "We had a big thunderstorm before you came, about four nights ago. It's gotten a good hold."

"Do you think we better get help?" Andrew said.

"I think we'll have to," Robin answered.

Sally shook her hair back. "The warden might see the smoke too, and come," she said.

"I doubt it," Robin said. "There's too much heat haze. We nearly fell in it ourselves before we saw it. Now listen." He looked at Sally. "You said you wanted to ride Swampfire . . ."

Sally felt her stomach go in her throat, partly with fear and partly with joy.

"If I start you on the path to the farm, you can follow it. It's easy—I'll tell you how."

"And I can get help, and Swampfire'll be safe from the warden," she finished.

"Right."

133

They ran back to the cabin and Robin untied Swampfire. He led him alongside the railing and Sally climbed on it, her heart pounding. The big horse edged away from the rail and his hindquarters swung out. Robin walked him around in a circle and tried again. This time Sally put her hand on Swampfire's back and he waited. She swung her leg over, feeling the silky red hairs under her thigh. Before she had time to lose her nerve, she gave a little jump and landed on his back.

She held her breath, wondering if he would bolt. Without a bit and bridle there was no way in the world they could hold him if he really wanted to run away. But he only backed up a little, and she gave a tentative little squeeze and push with her knees. He started forward, his neck high, his ears up. Robin jogged ahead, and Sally's throat was so tight it hurt. But all she did was sit up straight, trying to frown.

"How does it feel?" Andrew asked.

"Fine." She couldn't say any more. She wound one hand in the long silky mane and leaned forward. Swampfire speeded up, almost running Robin down. She sat back, her heart thumping, and he slowed his walk.

"Wow!" Andrew said. It was like seeing a horse in a movie, something not quite real.

"He's following you all by himself," Sally said. "I'm not doing a thing. Only my knees."

Robin stopped. He looped the rope over Swamp-fire's mane and tied the other end up on the halter. It made a kind of rein, except there wasn't any bit. "You'll have to neck rein him and shift your seat," he said. She hoped she could do it. Then Robin turned to Andrew. "Okay, hop up behind."

But Andrew shook his head. "Two of us can do a lot more here than one. I'll stay with you."

"You sure?" Robin stared at him.

Andrew nodded.

"Okay," was all Robin said, but Sally could tell how pleased he felt. Then Robin pointed to an opening in the trees. "Go through that and you're on the path," he said to Sally. "There's only one bad place, when it comes to a little lake. But don't worry about it; it's shallow. Just go straight across and pick up the trail on the other side. Oh, and there's a bog around that part, so stay on the path. You come out at the pasture, the same place we meet."

Sally nodded. She felt funny. She almost felt as though she needed Andrew. But so did Robin . . . better he stayed here. "See you," she said. She hoped they couldn't tell how nervous she felt.

She urged Swampfire forward and he immediately started to trot. She nearly fell off before she pulled him back to a walk. Coward, she said to herself. You ought to be galloping. You'll never get there this way.

She turned around. The boys were watching her.

She took a deep breath and leaned forward. It was now or never. "Come on, boy!" she whispered. She gripped with her knees and touched Swampfire with her heels. Instantly he lifted himself into a canter, his hoofs thudding across the clearing. At first Sally clutched onto him with her legs and her feet, even her hands on his neck. But then, as he rocked easily

along, she realized it wasn't going to be that hard to stay on, and she relaxed a little. She made herself sit back into his gait, shifting her body the way she wanted him to go. There was no time to look back or wave before they were entering the trees on the narrow path. She leaned forward again, concentrating on avoiding low branches. The vine reins were light and easy to hold, and for now she was all right. "Good boy," she whispered. They were on their way.

Robin and Andrew watched her disappear with a last flick of Swampfire's tail.

"That's done," Andrew said. "We should get to work."

"There's a shovel and a hoe in the back shed," Robin said. "You get them while I tell Pa what we're doing."

"Okay."

Robin found his father inside the cabin. "Pa, the swamp's burning."

His father straightened up, and Robin saw him wince with pain. "Bad fire?"

"I think so. It could be. Sally's gone for help."

The older man pushed himself out of the chair. "You go ahead. Start digging rings around it. I'll catch up."

When they got back to the trees, it seemed to Andrew the fires had grown. The columns of smoke were bigger, and he felt a momentary pang of fear. Suppose they couldn't stop it? But Robin was already working, using the tools they had brought to get down in the peat. Andrew bent to help him. This wasn't the time to start worrying about what might happen. A tiny breeze had sprung up, and it caught little flickers of fire and carried them out into the bushes. Robin and Andrew ran and put them out,

138

one after another, but it was impossible to find them all, and soon small ribbons of flame were fanning out into bigger blazes.

Andrew looked up and saw there was a section they had missed burning above ground. As they watched it crept out in a line that grew longer and longer, and Robin ran to it and chopped it out with his hoe just before it reached a small tree. Andrew went back along the fire with the shovel, turning burning pieces of peat over.

"Put this water on it," they heard a voice behind them. It was Robin's father, limping slowly toward them with a bucket. Robin ran to take it and threw the water on the flames. It seemed like a drop compared to what they needed.

"Is there any more water around I can get?" Andrew asked.

"The closest's the marsh, where I got this," Robin's father said. He leaned on his cane and studied the situation. "But buckets of water won't help. We'd need a cloudburst to get this out. Thing to do is cut it off, and we can do that with backfires. Now here's my plan. . . ." He found a stump and sat down painfully, pointing and explaining all the while. They listened carefully and then, feeling encouraged, they went to work again.

They lit the backfires, they beat at old flames and they shoveled dirt on new ones. Sometimes it seemed they were getting ahead. The trenches held in places, and one backfire stopped a whole blaze. And yet, when they dug into the peat beyond the trenches, they found the fire already burning. The breeze sent two backfires swerving sideways into new grass, and after an hour they had to admit the fire was gaining. Finally the older man stood up.

"The whole thing's going to bust out. There's a little time before it does, but not too long. Best we go back to the cabin; there's things to be done."

"Andrew can help you, Pa," Robin said. "Any extra I can hold it here, you'll have more time."

The man nodded. "All right. But don't be too long . . . don't get caught here."

"I won't," said Robin. He trotted off, the smoke quickly hiding him from view.

"My name is Andrew," Andrew said as they walked slowly back to the cabin. He thought maybe Robin's father hadn't heard his name when they first came. He noticed the smoke was following them.

"I know," the old man said. "The boy talked about you in the winter. You turned out better than I expected, too." He smiled at Andrew. "I like a boy who works as hard as you do. We almost stopped this fire ourselves, without any outside help. But now I guess we need it. I hope your sister's gettin' there all right."

Andrew stopped for a minute to wipe his face and smeared it black with his grimy hand. "She'll make it," he said. He cleaned his glasses with his smudgy shirt as he walked, and then he wiped his face with it. "That's the end of that shirt," he grinned.

Pa smiled back at him. "Reckon it won't hurt you none to have a dirty shirt. Shows you're a true fire-fighter."

When they reached the cabin Robin's father showed Andrew the well. "We'll get the blankets first, but we won't say what for. No point telling her yet . . . we may not have to." Andrew guessed he meant Robin's mother.

There were five blankets inside in a chest. They were wonderful colors, greens and oranges and blues. "She makes them for us," Pa said. "It keeps her busy with her hands."

"I hope we don't have to get them wet," Andrew said.

"We may have to wet them and our rugs too, if the fire gets close," Pa said. "We'll put them on the roof if we have to."

Andrew took them outside and put them in a pile by the well. Then he drove the cow up to the house and tied her, in case they needed to lead her off. He noticed Pa kept looking toward the marsh. They could see smoke now, rising thinly behind the scrub trees.

"Robin should have come by now," Andrew said. "I'll go see where he is."

"Good. And I'll see to my wife . . . get her ready to go, just in case."

"I'm sure it'll be okay," Andrew said. "My sister'll get help. I'm sure of it."

"I hope so," Pa said. "I'd hate to lose this cabin."

Andrew started back to Robin, wondering if Sally really was all right. She knew how to ride, but he didn't think she had ever ridden this way before, with only a vine halter and no saddle. He jogged faster, partly to hurry and partly to take his mind off the thought of what might happen if she fell off.

But Sally, far along the trail by now, was finding that Swampfire's canter had a natural rhythm, and it was almost easier to ride without a saddle. She thought they were making very good time. Straight, long stretches of trail opened up around every curve, each one an invitation to Swampfire to canter faster. His tail was flying back, the breeze was lifting Sally's hair, and if she hadn't been so worried about the fire, she would have felt completely free. She might have almost forgotten where she was and why she was riding.

The little lake had been easy, a splattering of water under Swampfire's curving feet. She saw the bog Robin had told her about. . . . It made her shudder, but they got past it, and then the long, white, sand trail laced with brown pine needles stretched ahead again. Swampfire was going just the way she had always dreamed a horse could be, wonderfully steady and yet with an easy speed that wasn't frightening.

Once he swerved at a flying squirrel that skittered through the air across the trail, but he recovered his stride in no time and Sally hardly joggled. "You're the most perfect horse in the world," she breathed.

Ahead lay a log, across the trail. Sally could feel Swampfire picking up slightly and she knew he was going to jump it. He sailed over with hardly a break in his stride, his mane curving over his neck and bouncing up and down like spun gold. She could feel his energy as he left the log behind like so much dust—a tremendous power underneath his relaxed way of going—and she wondered what it would be like if he were really running. Soon they were cantering on a gradual curve to the west, and it wasn't long before Sally saw light ahead through the trees. It came from open fields. "We're at the farm, Swampfire!" she said.

In a minute more they came out of the pines at the alder stream, and splashed through the water. Sally found the pasture gate—she had almost forgotten where it was because she and Andrew were used to scrambling over the fence—and opened it, and Swampfire flew up the hill toward the barns.

"Hey, we're back!" Sally called. She hoped the men would be working in the yard, but there was no sign of activity. The cows were gathered down below in the shade. The tractors were parked under the shed, which meant they weren't being used in the peanut fields. She slid off Swampfire's back and flipped the rope over a fence post. "Wait here, boy," she whispered. "I'll come right back."

She ran in the barn, but it was empty. She decided against putting Swampfire inside, in a cow stanchion. He probably wouldn't go in anyway, and it would take too much time. She ran back to him and undid the rein loop and tied the end of the rope to the fence post so he could graze. Then she raced through the barnyard and across the lawns. When she reached the house she rushed inside, calling Cousin Anne. A woman who sometimes helped with the housework was in the kitchen, canning tomatoes, and Sally was so glad to see her she almost fell on her.

"Mrs. Davis," she said. "Where is everybody? There's a fire in the swamp, they've got to come! Where's Cousin Anne?"

"She's gone to town." Mrs. Davis put down the glasses she was holding. "They all have. The conveyor belt broke and the men went to get it repaired, and your cousin went to get the vet. The bull's sick."

"Oh, no!" Sally said. "What'll I do?" She said it more to herself than to Mrs. Davis, but the woman noticed Sally's face. She went right over to the phone.

"Simple," she said. "We can call the fire department in town, and the game warden's office too."

"The game warden's already in the swamp," Sally said wearily. "But he doesn't know about the fire. He's not anywhere near it."

"Then his office will send some of the other men," Mrs. Davis said. She didn't seem to wonder how Sally knew where the warden was. She just went on dialing the town fire department. "Hello, operator? I want to report a fire." There was a pause, and she put her hand over the mouthpiece. "All those people work together in an emergency," she said. "I've seen it. My neighbor's woods caught fire once, and . . . hello, is that the fire department? Yes. I want to report a fire in the swamp. Yes, that's right . . . yes . . . out by Swamp Farm."

She went on talking, and Sally walked over to the window. She peered at the long line of trees below the pastures. She strained her eyes, and looked hard through the heat haze. She thought she saw a ribbon of smoke, and then she was sure. She ran back to Mrs. Davis, who was just hanging up. "Mrs. Davis, look! That's it! It's gotten bigger!"

"Now just calm down," Mrs. Davis said when she saw the smoke. "They'll get here pretty quickly. They can take care of it."

"But Andrew's back there!" Sally said. "And Robin, and Robin's house and his father and mother. I've got to go back!"

145

"I don't think you'd better," Mrs. Davis said. "Your Cousin Anne'd want you to stay here, out of danger. Wait till she gets back, anyway, or the men get here."

"No, I can't. I can't." Sally was already at the door. "Andrew's there. He's my brother, don't you understand. And he's younger than me. I've *got* to go."

She was down the porch steps and running, and hardly heard Mrs. Davis' protests following after her. She ran as she had never run, feeling first the lawn grass springing behind her flying feet and then the packed clay of the barnyard. She reached the fence and bolted over. Swampfire danced around on the end of the rope, whickering at her, his head high.

"Whoa, boy. You've got to be a good boy now, you've got to stand still by yourself." She was running her hand easily along the rope to his nose, patting him, undoing the other end. She led him quickly to the fence and climbed on it. He backed out, but she moved sideways on the fence and he came with her. For an instant his back was parallel with the top rail, and she jumped.

She landed with a thump. Swampfire gave a sailing leap forward that nearly threw her off, but she caught herself on his neck and hung on. He was galloping, out into the field, and Sally realized she had forgotten to loop the rope around to make a rein. She had only the end in one hand, and she felt a hot wave of panic. He was already in the middle of the huge pasture, and she knew if he kept going he would come to the five-foot rail fence. Sally was sure he would jump it like a bird, but she had never jumped high in her life.

She pushed herself back up to a sitting position and took a deep breath. "Whoa, boy," she said as calmly as she could. One ear flicked back and she thought she detected a change in his gait. She put her hand on his withers and pushed herself backward even more, sitting well down on his back. She pulled the rope and his head came around, and he began turning in a wide arc. "Whoa," she said again, and then again. His gallop was settling into a canter, and he was blowing and shaking his head. Finally he slowed to a trot, and Sally leaned to the left. To her relief, he turned.

I know how! she thought. I really know how to ride him! She felt like throwing her arms around his neck with a wild, shouting hug but she didn't dare; she might startle him again.

"You're a wonderful, wonderful horse," she whispered. "I'm going to love you forever."

At the gate he slowed and she slid off and fixed his rein, and led him through. She realized he didn't like being leaped on, and she mounted slowly, climbing first on the gate and then easing her way over on his back. This time he stood still, waiting until she picked up his reins and headed him across the stream. They took precious minutes finding the trail on the other side, but finally they pushed through some trees, and there it was.

"Hurry, Swampfire," she said. "The boys need us."

She tightened her knees and he began to canter again. Again there came that wonderful sensation of lightness, of floating free. She leaned forward even more, urging him to go as fast as she dared, flashing by the place where they had seen the flying squirrel, past the bog, through the little lake and on to the last stretch of trees near Robin's cabin. Sally lay glued almost flat on Swampfire's back, trusting him to see where he was going. The smell of smoke was in her nose now, getting thicker and more acrid every minute. So far she couldn't see any fire, and even when they came out at the cabin there were no visible flames yet, but black pillars of smoke rose in the air on the far side of the clearing.

"Hey!" she called. "Anybody home?"

Robin's father came on the porch. "They're at the fire," he said. "I was just going to see what's happened. Your brother went to get Robin, and now he hasn't come back either."

Sally's heart bumped with fear, but she shook it off. "I'll go," she said. "Swampfire's fast."

She had tightened her knees and he was already moving, picking his way around the marsh and can-

Now Sally could see the fire. She was horrified to see how much it had spread. It was in the open meadow and it seemed to be in a long line. There were smaller fires coming out in front and on either side, looking as though they had begun to spread into the scrub trees. If that happened, she knew there would be no possible way they could stop it. That's probably why the boys hadn't come back. They would be at one end or the other, trying to keep it out of the trees.

The fire was making Swampfire uneasy, but Sally gripped her knees tight and he kept going forward. "We can't chicken out now, Swampfire," she said. "We can't."

He edged warily closer, and Sally felt herself getting hot. She turned him a little way along the line to the right, and then to the left. Through the heavy smoke it was difficult to see. She was wondering where to start looking next when she heard a shout.

"Where are you?" she shouted back.

"Here!" It was Robin's voice, coming from her left. She moved Swampfire that way and then over the line of flames she saw Robin waving. It dawned on her that he shouldn't be on that side of the fire.

"Where's Andrew?" she called.

"He's here," Robin answered. "He's hurt his leg."

Sally's stomach lurched. "Oh, no," she muttered.

She heard Andrew's voice, saying his leg wasn't that bad. But now she knew why they weren't moving. They would have had to run to get through the fire, and if Andrew had hurt his leg he couldn't have gone fast enough.

"Did you bring help?" Robin shouted.

"Nobody was at the farm, but they're coming. We phoned the fire department."

There was a pause.

"I'll tell Pa," Sally went on. "We'll get you out somehow."

"Okay," Robin called. "We'll stay back and wait, but don't be too long. The fire's moving around behind us, too. Sally?" His voice sounded strange.

"What?"

"I think we're trapped," he said.

10

SALLY TURNED Swampfire around and they tore back through the smoke. Pa'll help, she said to herself. He'll know what to do. She must have been shouting, because Pa was waiting outside when she got to the cabin.

"What's happened?" Worry showed in his face.

She told him, and when she finished, his frown deepened. "If I could just ride, for five minutes . . ." His fists clenched. He shook his head, as though to clear his thoughts. "But I can't," he said more calmly. "So you'll have to."

"But what should I do?" Sally said.

"Use the horse," he answered. "The fire's not as big as you think, yet. If you hurry, you can still find a gap farther down, and carry them out. The horse can outrun the fire, where the boys can't."

"He's afraid of it," Sally said.

"Yes. But he won't panic if you don't." Pa's voice grew firm. "Anyway, no telling when help'll get here. There's nobody else but you."

Sally felt Swampfire backing up under her, and shaking his head up and down. Pa was right, of course, but how would she ever do it?

"Take this," Pa was pulling off his shirt. "If he shies off, cover his eyes and lead him. But get your brother on his back, and do it now."

Sally tied the shirt around her waist, and Pa gave her no chance to hesitate further. He smacked Swampfire's rump and the horse leaped forward, his back arched. Sally was so busy holding on she didn't have time to feel afraid, and by then Swampfire's canter straightened out and his back came down again. Once more she leaned into his stride and guided him back through the scrub trees. They came out into choking smoke, and Swampfire wheeled to the left, racing along the fire.

"Hey, Robin?" Sally shouted.

She heard his voice, directly opposite her. It was fainter than the last time. He must have moved farther back, and there was no opening at all here. She would have to go farther to find one.

"Come on, boy," she urged Swampfire. He snorted nervously, but he responded, galloping faster. Sally's eyes roved ahead, searching for an opening in the flames. We'll go all the way around if we have to, she thought. But after twenty yards she saw that the fire had cut across in front of them, blocking their path with a searing heat that made Swampfire wheel around again, his legs bunching under him. Sally felt him trembling and she realized that if she tried to stop him he would go out of control. She let him run back, past the place she had heard Robin, past the scrub trees, farther and farther away from the boys. Her eyes were smarting from the smoke, her throat was dry, and she felt almost ready to cry.

Then she saw something ahead. Not an opening, but at least a place in the woods where there was no fire. They came closer and she saw it was a tangled-looking thicket. At its far side was a huge fallen tree. The tree was still green, and its branches jutted up. Sally sat back and pulled on the reins, desperation giving her strength. Swampfire slowed, and she slid off almost before he stopped. Frantically she pulled at the fallen tree's branches, breaking off the ones she could and bending others down. If she could get it low enough for Swampfire to jump, they had a chance. Swampfire's ears flicked at her, but he kept turning to face the fires around them. She wondered if he understood what she was doing. "I know you can make it, Swampfire," Sally said.

It's me who probably can't, she thought, as she struggled back on him and turned to face the log.

Swampfire jogged under her, and for a minute she wavered. Suppose he refused? If she fell off and hurt herself, she couldn't reach the boys. But Swampfire was cantering, and she heard herself urging him to go faster. They were coming up on the log, and now they were right at it. She felt him check, pick himself up, and leave the ground. In the air she had a brief glimpse of the branches, and they were over. He had done it!

They cantered out of the thicket on the other side and turned left along a little red clay gulley. Huddles of frightened birds and rabbits were crouched along the bottom. Too dazed to run, they barely moved out of Swampfire's way, and Sally knew that if the fire wasn't stopped they would all be trapped here. The thought of getting trapped here herself suddenly seemed very real, and she shouted the boys' names.

They answered, dead ahead. Sally urged Swampfire out of the gulley and he breasted through high grass until Sally saw Robin standing by a clump of swamp cane. Andrew was sitting on the ground. One hand was on his leg below his swollen knee, the other was propping him up.

"It's only sprained," he said when she reached them.

"Don't get off," Robin said. He half lifted and half pushed Andrew up behind her. "Okay, go," he said. "Don't wait for me. I'll follow you."

Going back was easier. Swampfire had done it once, and he seemed to know the way. Twice Sally looked back and saw Robin, but the third time he had dropped behind. "Shouldn't you slow down so Robin can see you?" Andrew shouted in her ear.

"I can't," Sally said. "Swampfire's too nervous, and Robin said not to wait."

Swampfire checked for a moment when he saw the log, but he headed straight at it. Andrew's arms tightened around Sally's waist, and he wrapped his legs tight around the horse's belly. He bounced to one side as the horse picked up speed, but he got straight again. Swampfire's ears went forward as he came up on the jump, and they were over and out in a quick rush.

"What a horse!" Andrew said. They turned again to look for Robin, but there was no sign of him.

"Don't worry," Sally said, seeing Andrew's expression. "I'm going back as soon as I take you to the cabin."

"The marsh is closer," Andrew said. "And it's wet. That's safe enough."

"Okay," Sally said. "But if the fire gets near, lie in the water."

"Right."

Andrew slid off Swampfire beside a greenish-looking pool, and Sally only paused long enough to make sure he could manage on one leg. Every second counted now, and when she turned Sawmpfire back the horse galloped as though he knew it. Billows of smoke seemed like heavy fog all around them and the strange sky was turning darker. A tremor of fear ran over Sally's skin, and when she got to the fire she felt confused. There was no sign of Robin, and she couldn't find the fallen tree.

Then she realized why—it wasn't a low spot in the line any more. The fire had reached it, and now it was a wall of crackling flames, making a sound like the roaring ocean. For a second Sally was frozen with horror, and then her mind started working again. They would have to go farther, that's all. They would have to find another gap. Suddenly she saw Robin, running along on the other side. Through the flames she could see his arm rise in a panting wave, and she realized he had the same idea.

"I'm coming!" she called. "Keep going!"

It seemed the fire would never end, but terrified as she was, Sally could still marvel at Swampfire's speed. Again she felt that wonderful power, and even now she sensed that he still had plenty in reserve. Pa had been right: the horse was faster than the fire.

Finally they came to the spearhead of the line, and she turned him and they tore around the end. Robin was standing beneath a charred little tree, completely out of breath. When she reached him he caught Swampfire's halter and they turned and looked. The opening she had come through was still there, but it was shrinking fast.

"Oh, Robin," Sally said. "We'll never do it."

"Yes we will," Robin said. He jumped, and swung himself up in front of her. He leaned forward and patted Swampfire's neck. The horse was trembling. His ears were up, and he began to dance backward, shaking his head again and again.

"I've got Pa's shirt," Sally said. "He said cover his eyes and lead him."

"We don't have time," Robin said. "Hang on."

He put his hands high on Swampfire's mane and dug in his heels. Swampfire pawed the ground and turned this way and that. Somehow Robin kept him going forward, using his knees and the reins, never giving in to the horse's fear.

Sally's heart went in her throat. She held onto the sides of Robin's shirt. Hot gusts of air blew across their backs and faces, and she could hear the flames hissing. Swampfire whinnied and Robin slapped his flank hard with the end of the rope. "Go on, horse!" he said.

It was hard to breathe. Sally felt Robin's ribs going up and down as his lungs sucked for air, and her own eyes were stinging. She realized tears were streaming down her cheeks.

"Kick!" Robin said.

Swampfire edged sideways like a crab, but when

he felt their two sets of heels he almost dove forward. He half reared, and came down. Then he bolted. Sally closed her eyes tight and hung on, as Swampfire flashed into the fast-closing gap at a dead run. Branches cracked like rifle shots on every side, and showers of hot sparks swirled over them. The noise became a roar, and the furnacelike heat seemed to sear across their skin.

Suddenly the air got cooler. Sally opened her eyes. The fire was streaming away behind, and Swampfire was running as she had never felt anything run before, all of his power unleashed for this last, desperate effort. Blue sky appeared as they passed the worst of the smoke, and the air got cooler yet as the unburned greenery came toward them. Robin made no attempt to stop Swampfire, or even to guide him, but the hardwood trees were flowing into deep and spongy marsh, and when Swampfire reached the soft ground he slowed of his own accord. Twenty yards farther, and Robin was able to pull him to a stop.

"Oh-h-h," Sally's breath went out in a groan of relief.

Robin jumped off and patted Swampfire's lathered neck. "You're a good horse," he said. He said it over and over again. He turned around and Sally saw there were white ashes all through his hair. She was covered, too, with ashes and fine gray dust. Her legs felt so weak she didn't dare get down, so she lay along

Swampfire's neck and smoothed his mane until she stopped shaking. Then she slid off, and they both took handfuls of grass and tried to wipe the horse dry.

"That's the fastest I've ever been in my life," Sally said. "Running, I mean."

"Me too," Robin said. "Seems like he's a race horse." He threw down his grass. "That's enough for now. We can cool him down walking through the marsh. We better move. The fire's still coming."

They looked for Andrew at the marshy pool, but he had left it. An arrow made of twigs was lying on the moss, pointing to the cabin. Andrew was halfway there when they caught up with him, using a sturdy forked stick for a crutch. At their shout he turned around, and when he saw them a big smile spread over his face.

"Boy," he said. "I was really scared about you. I was going for Pa."

"Hop on," Robin said. "We're all going."

"I've been hearing an engine noise, too," Andrew said as they boosted him up on Swampfire. "Like a plane or something."

In a minute they heard it again. Sally tilted her head back. "It's a helicopter!" she said.

Instinctively Robin ducked. "The warden," he said. "He said he was sending for one, at the lake."

They watched the helicopter speed in from the east in a wide circle over the fire. The children almost expected it to swerve and circle the way a bird would, but it slanted straight down with its rotors clattering, and disappeared in the smoke before they could see where it landed. But not before they saw the faces and shapes of six or seven men inside, wearing khaki jump suits.

"It could be the fire department," Sally said. "The people Mrs. Davis called."

"Boy, they look like they mean business," Andrew said.

"I hope so." Sally was thinking of all the trapped animals she had seen.

"Let's get back to the cabin," Robin said. "Pa'll be wondering where we are."

"Good idea, I'm starvi—" Andrew stopped, an embarrassed look on his face.

Robin grinned. "I remember I invited you to eat," he said. "After we hide Swampfire."

He led them through the scrub trees until they were on the opposite side of the clearing from the fire, near the path to Swamp Farm. They tied Swampfire to a bush, and peered out. The men were ahead of them. The helicopter was parked in the cow lot, and there was a firefighter on the cabin porch. Robin jumped back, and pulled Swampfire farther into the trees.

"I'll go see what's happening," he said. "Wait here."

He darted out in the sunlight, zigzagging to the cabin. Andrew shifted on Swampfire's back, and he made a face from the pain in his knee.

"How'd you hurt it?" she said.

"I was running, and I stepped in a hole. It was really dumb."

He looked gloomy, sitting on top of the horse with his leg jutting out and the afternoon sunlight glinting off his hair. Sally suddenly had a funny feeling about him. She couldn't remember when she had felt like that before. It must have been a long time ago, when he was little. Maybe when he was learning to tie his shoelaces, or the time she helped him learn the alphabet.

"It was really good the way you fought the fire," she blurted out.

Andrew's face got all open with looking pleased. "Thanks," he said. His expression showed only long enough for her to know how much her opinion mattered, even though most of the time, he tried not to show it.

They heard Ghoster barking, and Swampfire snorted. Robin was jogging across the clearing toward the trees. He angled away from where they were until he got in the woods, and then he hurried toward them.

"What's happening?" Andrew said.

"Two of them were inside, so I had to hide. They

were asking Pa questions." Robin took pieces of corn bread and hard chunks of smoked ham out of a food sack and handed them around.

"What did Pa say?" Andrew stuffed the ham in his mouth.

"Nothing about Swampfire," Robin said. "He only told about the fire."

"Hey, this is really good." Sally was munching corn bread. "What're the men doing now?"

"He said he thinks they can hold the fire, but they've called for more men. They've got packs on their backs with hoses," Robin said.

Andrew helped himself to more ham. "Probably foam sprayers."

Robin got up. "I think we should take Swampfire to the farm. We can go now, while they're busy," he said. "Pa says he can manage till I get back."

"Okay." Andrew stopped eating and straddled Swampfire again, patting him. They noticed his knee had swelled.

Sally got up and straightened her torn shorts. A spider had run down her collar and was crawling on her shoulder blade. She got it out and flung it off. "This has been one of the busiest days of my life," she said.

Robin decided they should walk parallel to the path, and he put Sally in front leading Swampfire, while he followed behind as a rear guard. The firefighters seemed far away, but it was better not to take chances.

They walked this way until they crossed the little lake. On the other side, the ground off the trail looked dangerous, with dark pools and queer looking mud, and Robin went back to the path. It widened out, and started to curve. Suddenly Swampfire stopped. His ears pricked ahead.

"Pull him off the trail," Robin hissed. "Someone's up there."

But it was too late. Around the bend came Cousin Anne. Two of her farm helpers were with her, and behind came two more men that the children didn't know. They wore khaki uniforms, like the warden's. Cousin Anne was wearing rubber boots and a raincoat, and she looked hot. When she saw them she stopped dead.

Andrew waved. "Hi," he said. "We were just coming to check in, the way you said. Every other day."

"Check *in*," Cousin Anne said. She sounded upset. "What in the world is going on? Mrs. Davis said you were trapped in the fire."

"We were," Andrew said. "But Sally got us out. We're fine." He smiled at her.

"And we found the ghost," Sally said, patting Swampfire. "Isn't he beautiful?" She started to explain, but Cousin Anne shook her head.

"Tell me later," she said. She came closer and

peered at them. "Are you really all right?"

"Sure."

But Cousin Anne had seen Andrew's swollen knee. She ran her hand over it. He tried not to wince, but he couldn't help it.

"Go back to the farm at once," Cousin Anne said. "The vet's at the barn with the bull—he can look at that leg until I get a doctor."

"We told you, that's where we were going," Sally said.

"I hope so," Cousin Anne said. "And after I see about this fire we're going to have a serious talk."

She marched off, her back looking stiff, and the children watched until they were all out of sight.

"Did you see the way those guys looked at Swampfire?" Andrew said. "Now what'll we do?"

"What Cousin Anne says," Sally said. "Go to the farm, and see the vet. After she calms down, she'll let us explain."

"What good will explaining to her do?" Andrew said irritably. "She's not Swampfire's owner."

"That's right, but those men aren't either, and she won't let them take him."

"I meant his real owner," Andrew said.

"Oh, shut up, Andrew," Sally said. "He doesn't have one. He wouldn't have been in the swamp if he did."

"Of course he does," Andrew said. "How do you

think he got there in the first place?"

"I don't know, but we got him out. He'd be permanently lost if we hadn't, so I think that makes him ours." To her amazement she felt her eyes filling with tears, but she stared defiantly at the boys anyway. They stared back at her, as upset as she was.

Robin broke the silence. "We can't cross each other, not now."

"Okay," Andrew said.

Sally started walking again, shaking her head so the tears fell away and she could see.

"Maybe it would be better if I take Swampfire with me and hide him, somewhere in the swamp," Robin said.

"That's not a bad idea." Andrew shifted, letting both legs hang sideways. "Especially if you didn't tell us where. Then if Cousin Anne asked us, or the warden, we could say we don't know. Even if they tortured us."

"No," Sally said. "Then he wouldn't be with us, and we'd always be hiding him. Anyway, they've seen him now."

This was so true that there was no answering it, and they walked on in silence, the last of the swamp brooding around them. Sally breathed its smells and remembered what an impossible idea it had been to find Swampfire, only two days ago. And now they were bringing him home, and they had camped out in the swamp besides.

"I wish it wasn't now," she said finally. "I mean, I wish they hadn't invented cars yet. Horses used to be so much more important. If we lived a hundred years ago we could be bringing home an animal that our parents would be thrilled to get, instead of worrying about keeping him."

"My Pa would want him, if he was a work horse," Robin said. "But he's too fine."

"He's great for riding." Andrew sprawled back on Swampfire, feeling the muscles move against his backbone as the horse walked. Then he sat up again because a big black and red bird flew over their heads across the trail. "Hey, I think that's an ivory-billed woodpecker!" he shouted. "They're supposed to be extinct!"

Everyone looked back into the trees where the bird had disappeared. In a minute they heard his "rat-tat-tat" break the silence. It sounded just like a riveter.

"Well, they're not," Sally said, feeling goosebumps up her spine, "if we just saw one."

Andrew craned his neck, making sure of the place. "I wonder where his range is."

"Somewhere back in the swamp," Robin said. "The fire drove him out here."

"I hope he stays so I can come back with my camera," Andrew said. "People never believe children."

He rode looking backward for a long while, and

then he heard Robin say, "There's a truck."

They had come to the farm. They could see the pickup parked across the stream, at the bottom of the pastures, and they saw the U.S. Forestry Service emblem on its door.

"That's those guys that were with Cousin Anne," Andrew said.

"It's empty," Robin said. "Come on."

"We've got to figure out a good place to put Swampfire," Sally said.

"How about that stall on the back side of the barn?" Andrew said. "You can't see it from anywhere, that old peach tree hides it."

"Good idea." Sally pushed her hair out of her eyes. "We can clean it up and nobody'll know."

They came up through the pastures without seeing anyone, and found the vet at the barn just getting ready to leave. He let out a low whistle when he saw Swampfire.

"Nice horse," he said. "I didn't know Miss Annie had one."

Andrew thought quickly. "Oh, uh, she just got him."

The vet nodded. "You kids must be having fun with him, if he's not too much for you. Show stock, isn't he."

It was more a statement than a question, and something clicked in Sally's mind. Some remembered pictures from a horse book—the finely drawn head, the chiselled legs, the long forelock. What did show stock mean? Maybe it explained Swampfire's courage, and his speed.

"Hey, what happened?" The vet noticed Robin was helping Andrew walk. "Here, let me see you."

"I hurt my knee," Andrew said. "It's not bad, though."

The vet stretched out Andrew's leg with gentle hands, probing everywhere until he was satisfied.

"You've torn a ligament," he said. "Nothing serious, but you'll be out of commission for a couple of weeks. I'll put a stretch bandage on it and we'll get you some crutches in town. How'd you do it?"

While Andrew told him, the vet got out the bandage, which was huge because it was meant for a cow, and wrapped it around Andrew's knee. Then he packed up his bag and looked around. "Where'd the others go?"

Andrew shrugged. "Out, I guess."

"I wanted to get a better look at the horse," the vet said. "Oh, well, some other time." He got ready to leave. "I'll send the crutches out in the morning. Keep off your leg until they get here, and, if it doesn't feel better in a few days, have Miss Annie's doctor look at it. But I think you'll be fine."

"Okay," Andrew said. "Thanks."

The vet waved and drove away, and Andrew

hopped around the barn to the back, where Robin and Sally were spreading fresh straw in Swampfire's stall.

"He's gone," Andrew said. "He didn't ask any more." Andrew patted Swampfire's neck and sat on a box, watching Robin wash him down with a sponge and a bucket of water. Sally found an old currycomb, and struggled to comb out his mane and tail, until they hung in long glistening cascades of silver. They got some hay and put it in the feed rack, and brought him more water to drink. Then Robin led him into the stall and closed the door. Swampfire walked forward and looked at them.

"He's tended to now. I don't think he'll fret," Robin said.

"He likes it," Andrew said.

"I've got to go," Robin turned around. "I'll be here as early as I can tomorrow."

Sally hung over the stall door, watching Swampfire eat, not wanting to leave him. "We've done it," she said. "We've rescued the ghost."

Robin grinned, and walked out to the top of the hill. "More like he rescued us," he said.

11

"THE FIRE's out," Andrew and Sally heard the warden say to Cousin Anne. He was in the Swamp Farm
sitting room and Sally and Andrew were standing
in the upstairs hall. "Or just about. Maybe one or
two places left, but my men are mopping 'em up
now. Where're the kids?"

The last of the afternoon sunlight was filling the
house. Sally heard Cousin Anne come into the hall
to call them. Andrew got up from the top step, where
he had been trying to eavesdrop, and hopped behind
Sally down into the parlor. The warden was in the
middle of the room, seeming to touch the ceiling.
When they came in he began talking to Cousin Anne
again.

"I ought to be mad, but I'm not. These kids did a
good job. If it wasn't for the work they did, trenches

and all, that fire would of took off much sooner'n it did. That cabin would be gone. Darn near all the growth, too. No, we'll just call it a standoff. But—" he turned and faced them with the full glare of all six-foot-two of him—"if you *ever* take off with my boat again . . ." his words stopped, but his tone went right through them. For a second Andrew was almost glad there had been a fire because it had kept the warden from looking for them.

"We won't," Sally said. "We're sorry."

"Right," Andrew said.

"Okay, that's it." The warden turned and clomped out. "Ghosts," they heard his growling voice drift back. "Ghosts."

Sally and Andrew looked at each other.

"He didn't say anything about Swampfire!" Sally said. "Does that mean we can keep him?"

"I have no idea what will happen," Cousin Anne said firmly. "The warden's put out an alert, and he'll let us know when he hears something."

"But what would he hear?" Sally said. "Swampfire couldn't belong to anybody. He was living in the swamp."

"This isn't the wild West, with horses running around loose," Cousin Anne answered. "The creature belongs to somebody, and you have no right to other people's property. But it may take a while to find out who the owner is, so for now you might as well relax and eat supper." She walked into the dining room.

But Sally didn't move. "I don't feel hungry," she said.

Cousin Anne sat down and started ladling food on their plates the way she always did. "Well, nobody's claimed him yet," she said. "Wait till someone does before you get all riled up, so you know where to put yourself. And it won't hurt you to take time out to eat, after all that's happened. I'm surprised you weren't scared to death in that swamp."

"We were," Andrew admitted.

"But we got over it," Sally said. She came in the dining room and sat down.

"You'd better start at the beginning, and tell me what you did," Cousin Anne said. "So we can get it all straightened out. When did you get lost?"

"That's the amazing part," Andrew said. "We were never lost."

"What we were doing was hiding," Sally said. "You see . . ." She began to tell Cousin Anne about the first night they were camping, when they heard the hounds, and as she talked she began to feel better, and she picked up her fork and started eating. She described their trip to the meadow, and the wildcat, and how she felt when she saw Swampfire for the first time.

Andrew explained how the warden came, and followed them, and why they couldn't bring Swampfire back by the canal. He told about their long trek to Lake Drummond, and building the platform. Neither one of them mentioned their terror, or the bear. But they remembered it, and outside as the dark came and the moon rose, it seemed good to be back in a house, with lights, and beds, and food that was cooked on a stove. They ate and talked, and ate and talked, and when they finished Cousin Anne pushed her chair back.

"Now I understand," she said. "Most of it, anyway. I can see why you went after that horse, even though it was heedless. It would have taken an extra hour for one of you to come back and tell me, but it would have been far more responsible."

"But we were with Robin," Sally said.

"And you wouldn't have let us go," Andrew said.

She looked at him, a stern expression on her face. "You don't know what I would have done. That's *my* business; to make a decision."

There was a long minute's silence. Sally and Andrew looked at their plates. Then she spoke again, and she sounded very serious.

"All right. Now that it's all happened the way it has, I've decided to let it go, this one time. I want you to learn from your experiences, and in this case I think you have. As long as you remember to never, *never* again do anything that's dangerous, without telling somebody else." She paused, and then she said,

"Now look at me. I love having you here in the summertime, but if you expect to continue to be here, you'll keep my rules. I can't have it any other way. Do you understand?"

They nodded. They could tell she meant it.

Cousin Anne got up and walked out into the hall. "I feel the same way you do about that horse. . . . I wish I knew where he came from. I want to take a good look at him in the morning, but right now I want you, Andrew, off that knee." She pointed upstairs. "You're both going to bed."

"Could I check on Swampfire first, just to make sure he's okay?" Sally said. "He's not used to the stall."

"All right, but be quick. The big flashlight is in the back hall cupboard."

Cousin Anne's big electric lantern cast a reassuringly wide circle of light as Sally walked down to the barn. The heat had faded, and the dew was forming on the fields. Sally could smell honeysuckle. It was very different from last night; the only animal noises were a sleepy chorus of clucks coming from the chicken house, and low moos from the cows standing close to the fences, comfortably chewing their cuds. Sally came around the barn past the peach tree and saw Swampfire's head poking out of his stall door. He saw her too and whuffled at her, a soft friendly sound.

Sally stroked his velvety nose. His breath felt warm and the stall already had a wonderful smell of horse. She closed her eyes and breathed it in, while a barn cat rubbed its way around her legs. Sally leaned against the wood planks and stared down the hill toward the swamp. It looked as mysterious as ever in the moonlight, and it still seemed hard to believe they had found Swampfire in all that vast expanse, and been able to bring him home.

"Maybe we really were lucky, Swampfire," she murmured, smoothing his long forelock. "And maybe we'll still be lucky, and nobody'll come for you."

But walking back to the house through the dappled shadows of moonlight, she didn't feel very sure. If the warden found Swampfire's owner, she knew he wouldn't hesitate to take Swampfire and give him back. Sally sighed. Robin was probably right; they should have hidden Swampfire, deep in the swamp. Well, it was too late now. They would just have to hope that no one came forward to claim him.

She climbed the stairs and Cousin Anne came out of her room and gave Sally a hug.

"I'm glad you're back," she said.

"So am I," Sally answered. At least I guess I am, she thought.

Andrew was in their room hanging over the window sill. He turned around when she came in. "You know, I've been thinking," he said. "How much we learned. We could probably survive anywhere, after today."

"Umn." Sally went over to her bed. Her mind was still on Swampfire.

"Except I'll never know as much as Robin," Andrew went on. "Even if I was in the swamp all summer."

"You already know a lot of things, just not the same ones he does," Sally said. She got up and started walking around the mattress, trying to balance on the balls of her feet. "Do you think he feels bad about his mother?" she said.

"Sure," Andrew said. "Wouldn't you?"

"Yes, but he doesn't seem to. He seems happy."

"Well, she makes things, and they like her. They have a neat house." Andrew yawned and hopped to his bed. "I like his father."

"Same." Sally's foot slipped and she fell to the floor with a crash. She got up and got in bed.

Andrew didn't say any more, and Sally lay there, thinking. It was funny how people could be so good at some things and so embarrassed about others. Robin knew more about the swamp than they did, but by now she knew that he couldn't say his feelings out, either through his words or even showing them the way he really wanted.

She looked over at Andrew. She saw why he hadn't answered her. He was already asleep, his bandaged knee propped up on a pillow. She stretched. Even though she was tired, she wasn't quite ready to go to sleep yet. She wondered what Robin was doing. She imagined him sitting in the clearing in the moonlight, patting Ghoster. Her mind drifted to the meadow, where they had first seen Swampfire's hoofprints, and she fell asleep dreaming of a herd of wild horses, living in the meadow, and all looking exactly alike.

When Andrew woke up the sun was already high. Andrew didn't know where he was until he moved, and then he felt a pain in his knee, and knew. He sat up and found his bird book, looking for ivory-billed woodpeckers. They were there, and the book said, "probably extinct." He was almost sure that was the bird he had seen, unless it had been a pileated woodpecker. Still, he had all summer to look for it, and he felt so excited he got up and hobbled to the window.

It was one of those mornings that, when you were in school in the winter, was hard to even imagine. Indoors on a cold snowy day, you couldn't remember the green and the blue, and the sunlight. And how fresh-washed it was, and how the warm air seemed to connect you to everything. Andrew looked along the hill to the pigpens, and the chicken house. They looked the same—as though nothing had happened. He could see the barn, and he wondered if Swampfire was all right.

"Sally?" he said.

She mumbled in her sleep.

"It's today," Andrew said. "Wake up."

She sat up and then she jumped up. "I'll go see if he's okay." She dashed into the bathroom to get dressed, and ran out again combing her hair. "You stay here. Cousin Anne won't like it if you walk."

She clattered down the steps two at a time and disappeared, and Andrew went back to the window. A car came through the gates and he saw it was some of the farm men, coming to work from town. He watched it come up the long driveway, and slow down for three fat geese that waddled in front of it. He decided that when he grew up he was going to have a farm. The car came around the house and the men got out, and one of them was carrying a pair of crutches. Andrew pulled on his clothes and bumped himself down the stairs on his seat, and hopped to the back door.

He was starting to try the crutches out up and down the front walk, when Sally came back from the barn.

"Swampfire's fine," she said. "I fed him. Can I try?"

"Sure. It's easy, you just have to sort of swing your legs."

They practiced until breakfast and then again until Cousin Anne was ready to go to the barn. While they were walking past the shed, Sally saw one hawk flying over the pasture, and she poked Andrew. "Look," she said. But she didn't say any more, and Andrew was puzzled.

"Do you think it's a good sign?" he whispered.

"I don't know," she said. "I hope so."

At Swampfire's stall Cousin Anne peered over the door, but it was shadowy inside and hard to see. "You might as well bring him out so we can take a good look at him," she said.

Sally led him out. "Isn't he beautiful?" she said, stroking Swampfire's shining neck. It felt hard and muscled beneath her touch, and she ran her hand through his thick mane.

"He certainly is," Cousin Anne said. "It's been many a year since I've seen a horse like that."

She walked all around him to admire him, while Sally straightened his vine halter. It looked scruffy in the bright sunshine.

"Is that what you led him by?" Cousin Anne said. "Goodness me, he could have broken that any time he wanted to. He must have wanted to stay with you."

She dug around in the barn and found an old leather bridle. "You can ride him better with this," she said. She was just handing it to them when Mrs. Davis appeared in the doorway and told Cousin Anne she was wanted on the phone.

Sally's throat tightened. "Who is it?" she said.

Mrs. Davis looked surprised. "I don't know . . . didn't ask."

Sally put Swampfire back in the stall, and she and Andrew trailed after Cousin Anne up to the house, and waited outside the kitchen door. "Wish on the hawks," Sally said. "Wish hard."

Then Cousin Anne pushed open the screen.

"That was the State Police," she said. "They found the owner."

Sally felt strange. The top of her head started pounding. Her face got hot.

"Who?" Andrew said.

"A woman who lives in Suffolk," Cousin Anne said. Name's Mrs. Cary. She's driving over this afternoon."

"How do they know Swampfire's hers?" Andrew said, while Sally struggled not to burst into tears.

"Can I call Mom and Dad?" Sally finally got her voice steady. "If I can talk to them before she gets here, maybe they'll let us offer to buy him."

Cousin Anne ran her hand over the top of Sally's head. "You don't understand," she said. "Seems this is the third time he's run away, and the woman wants to talk to us about keeping him here. She figures if you could catch him in that swamp, holding on to him would be easy."

"Keeping him here?" Sally repeated.

"That's right," Cousin Anne smiled at her. "I don't know how it'll work out, but she's coming over to talk about it. It sounds all right to me."

Sally flung her arms around Cousin Anne's neck.

"I can't believe it!" she said. "Did she tell you any more about him?"

"Yes. She says her husband is in the Navy and he sent the horse home to her from North Africa, as a present. That's why she doesn't exactly know what to do with him. He's a full-blooded Arabian."

"Wow!" Andrew said.

"It's the hawks!" Sally said. "I know it's the hawks."

"Well, I'm glad, whatever it is," Cousin Anne said. "But if I don't get back to my work this whole farm'll fall apart. If you haven't got anything to do until she gets here, I can give you some work, too."

"Oh, we have," Sally said. "Robin's coming and we've got to check on our camp, and . . ." She saw Cousin Anne was smiling.

"All right," Cousin Anne said. "Make some sandwiches and go, but just don't stay too long. I'll ring the big bell when Mrs. Cary comes." She went in the house.

Sally gave a jump, smelling the thick grass and feeling the hot sun. "Think of it," she said. "A real Arabian."

"They're a definite breed," Andrew said. "I'll have to buy a horse book." They started walking slowly back to the barn. Already the fields were getting white hot, and they kept to the deep green shade trees along the lawn.

"Maybe we could put him in horse shows," Sally said.

"Or even races," Andrew added. "I can be the jockey."

"You eat too much to be a jockey." Sally hitched up her shorts.

"Umn." He had to agree. It would be hard to be really thin, even for Swampfire.

"I hope he doesn't get tired of us, and run away from here, too," Sally said.

"He won't." Andrew picked up an ear of corn and propped his crutches against the barn fence. He climbed on the top rail and started shelling the corn in his hand. "He likes us more all the time. You can tell. Look at him."

Swampfire was poking at Sally's elbow, wanting the sugar she had brought from breakfast. She opened his door and went in. He sniffed in her pocket and she giggled because it tickled. Andrew hung over the door and fed him the corn, and Swampfire blew it all over his hand.

Sally wiped him off with a rag, and then Andrew helped her get his bridle on. Sally looked around, feeling a surge of joy. The whole day was waiting for them, out in the fields.

"Let's ride down and wait for Robin by the stream," she said.

"Okay."

Andrew got on from the top rail, easing his crutches on his lap. Sally climbed on in front. She jiggled the reins and Swampfire rolled the bit around in his mouth. The bridle seemed heavy, and she thought she had liked the halter better. She decided she would go back to using it after this.

They went past the pigpens and the orchard, and then they turned down the hill. Swampfire's snort was a cheerful sound this morning, while Delilah ranged around him, flushing speedy rabbits out of the blackberries along the edge of the fence.

"I wonder if she's ever caught one," Sally said.

"Probably not," Andrew grunted. He was having trouble holding on, because Swampfire had bounced into a trot.

"We'd better either canter or walk," he said.

Sally pulled Swampfire back and they angled down the field to the stream. They got off and Andrew sat on a moss bank, his feet in the water. It was hot, even in the shade. Suddenly he whooped, and Sally jumped.

"What's the matter?" she said.

He was on his hands and knees, digging frantically in a patch of grass. He held his treasure up at her—a beautiful, long, pointed rock, with a groove running all the way around its tapered thick end. "Arrowhead?" Sally said.

"Even better. A spearhead." He got to his feet.

"They must have camped here."

He hopped off along the stream, finding four perfect arrowheads as he went, but Sally didn't move. The arrowheads were exciting, but somehow she didn't feel as interested in Indians as she had before. She didn't really think she wanted to be living with a mother and father and family that all wore skin clothes and moccasins, in a tent. It was better like this, with the swamp nearby and the house up on the hill too, just in case. Besides, what would Andrew have done? In the old days Indians didn't have glasses. He would have hated it, if he had wanted to watch the birds and couldn't find them, or look at anything else he wanted to study.

Sally felt queer, like a person seeing two things at once, and somehow big and ashamed at the same time. Maybe you should stay in your own life, and not wish you were somebody else. It might not be as good as you thought.

She stretched out on the stream bank. Swampfire was cropping the grass nearby, and Sally could hear the crunches as he took strong bites. Her back itched. She turned over and saw the ground she had been lying on was covered with tiny bugs. She shuddered and rolled near the water and lay there, listening to Andrew hopping back.

"Look." Andrew dropped the arrowheads on the grass beside her. Sally picked them up, feeling their smoothness. They looked like jewels, especially made for the grass.

"We forgot to make the sandwiches," Andrew said.

"We can get them later," Sally said. "I'm not going back now."

"But I'm starved," Andrew said.

"You're always starved." Sally got up. "I want to wait for Robin."

They heard a noise. Robin had come without their knowing and he was standing across the stream, laughing. His breath was coming out in gasps, and they stopped arguing and stared at him.

"It's your fighting," he said between breaths. "You're always doing it."

"We like to," Sally said.

"I know," he said. "That's what's so funny."

Something about knowing made him feel good, and he jumped up and grabbed a branch and swung across the stream, and landed with a thump. They ran over and told him about Mrs. Cary.

"That's fine," he said. "That's really fine." They could see in his face how pleased he was.

"How's Pa?" Andrew asked. "And your mother."

"Fine. Pa says for you to come back again, sometime."

"Say, thanks," Andrew said. "We will."

"Robin," Sally said. "Shouldn't we check the camp? The hammocks, and all our stuff, and everything?"

Robin nodded. "That's what I was thinking," he said. "And I saw a crayfish in the stream. We could try to catch it and cook it for lunch."

"What about your canoe?" Andrew said. "How're we going to get it?"

"I thought we'd best build another one," Robin said. "To take us to the meadow. Then we'll have an extra one. For you." He looked at Andrew. "You can ride around in it until your knee is well."

"Hey, that's great!" Andrew burst into a smile. "I can help you make it. Let's go to the camp and start planning."

"Come on." Sally climbed on a stump and scrambled on Swampfire's back. His neck arched, and his ears went forward. She gathered up his reins. At that moment a hound bayed somewhere off in the swamp, a wild and wonderful sound against the sunlight, speaking of dark spaces under trees, pulling them back into lush meadows, deep into the green thickets.

"Ghoster," Robin said. "He's after something."

Andrew collected his crutches. "Aren't you glad it's not us," he said, and Robin smiled.

"Oh, I don't know," Sally said. Swampfire stood there waiting, huge and strong beneath her legs. She leaned forward, and he began to move. "Somehow I don't think I'd mind if he was."

THE AUTHOR

PATRICIA CECIL HASS divides her time between Green-
wich, Connecticut, where her husband is an executive
with a major food corporation, and Washington, D.C.,
where she is active in the production of television films
for children. In between, with their three children, they
spend as much time as possible at the 300-year-old
family property in Virginia, "Old Mansion" (the real
Swamp Farm). There they pursue their hobbies of riding and farming.

THE ILLUSTRATOR

CHARLES ROBINSON has been illustrating books for children since 1968 when he gave up practicing law. He
has received many awards for his work, including in
1971 the Gold Medal of the Society of Illustrators. He
and his wife and three children live in New Vernon,
New Jersey.